Awakening from a
Distant Dream

by
Joseph Aprile

Joseph Aprile

ISBN 978-8182530003

Second Edition

Artwork by Joseph Aprile

Other Books by the Author

- At the Fringes of Experience - Collection of Novellas
- America and the Mythology of Greatness - Non-fiction
- Impaled on Time's Illustrious Arrow - Poetry
- The Surprising Latitude of Fate - Novel
- The Illusive Quality of Existence - Poetry
- The Human Equation -Short Stories
- A Particular Passing Through Time - Novel
- Voices for Peace and Social Justice - Non-Fiction
- The Life and Times of Jeremy Sykes - Novel
- Daydreams and Other Lapses - Poetry
- The Human Equation Vol. II – Stories & Essays
- Voices for Peace and Social Justice Vol. II - Non-Fiction

These works are available for purchase at many sites including Amazon.com and Lulu.com

Awakening from a Distant Dream

Dedication

For my wife and life's companion, Julia, whose patience, understanding and generous assistance has made this book possible.

Laura

The three o'clock bell rang and Laura felt a great relief pass through her; she was looking forward to the end of another excruciating day of what she regarded as pointless classes. She automatically and quickly gathered up her books. For a brief moment, she paused and looked about her. All her classmates, who had only moments before seemed to be in a vegetative-like state now became animated as if mysteriously. This renewed biological vigor was focused towards the exit door. "How weird," she thought. She felt strangely sick at heart. The source of this feeling was unknown to her. It frightened her, and made her feel uncomfortable. Ordinary reality often made such a deep impression upon her, invading her composure, making her feel off balance and vulnerable. Laura's capacity to view the world around her so critically sometimes gave her cause to doubt her own sanity.

Outside the gray and formidable structure of school, the air was ripe with the scents of fall. Laura felt a close kinship with this season. It somehow was a reflection of a dark and voluptuous nature as of yet to be discovered. Laura felt that this season was her very own - a glorious brooding companion that encompassed the death of itself. The road that led back to her house was long and winding. She longed to watch the leaves in their mosaic beauty and capture their vividness forever in her memory.

For long moments, her heart seemed to stop beating, her lungs quieted and her feet took root in the wet loam. She felt herself becoming transformed into a beautiful thing of the forest discharging its fragrance into the air. She captured the sun in her myriad branches and held it there. She became endless and purely alive with no aspirations or fears to haunt or discourage her. Suddenly, however, the spell was broken by an image of her human self: unsteady on two feet, awkward, timid and alone with her shoulders

Awakening from a Distant Dream

slightly stooped and her head solemnly oriented towards the earth below her feet.

Laura approached her home. She knew the rooms, the windows, the closets, the old furniture, the vinyl dinette set with a Formica veneer, the ornate lamps with the plastic still covering the lampshades and most of all the television, a one-eyed despot sitting in its illustrious place of honor.

In her mind, Laura envisioned everything that transpired behind the front door of her house - her mother sprawled on the living room sofa with a heavy sedative containing alcohol thinly disguised in a coffee cup, and the television, of course, mercilessly on. She saw with perfect clarity the vacant eyes, the immobile features, the impenetrable life of this woman, her mother. Laura felt her skin tighten; she instantaneously felt all the obvious and subtle side effects of anxiety inundate her as her hand reached automatically for the door. In a moment, everything was revealed exactly as the mind's eye had portrayed it. An involuntary spasm shook Laura's entire frame, as she pretended, at great cost to herself, that everything was as it should be. Her mind frantically engaged its most obsessive urge to construct an image of an orderly universe, and shaped from the immediate reality a sense of normalcy upon which she could base the calm behavior she sought to feign. "Laura," she admonished herself within the inner parliament of her being, "you know that this is the way the game is played, you know your role, play it well." That was the voice of the pragmatist attempting to coexist with her mother without giving way to the dangerous volatility of the psyche. In this way, she regained her composure. However, somewhere anger was stored inside her, piled up in meticulous heaps leaving microscopic regions of stress throughout her physical being.

"Hello mother," she said as she entered the house. A long and painful silence intervened.

Laura

Her mother barely stirred as the light from the television gave her complexion the ivory color of death. She swiveled her head about a broad neck, "Oh, hello dear," was her reply, each word chosen carefully and articulated with painful slowness. "How was your day?"

Laura stood there aware of everything. She understood that her mother did not really require or desire a thorough and honest response to this question. "Oh all right mother." The tension rose in her once again. She moved stiffly towards the kitchen. Laura was one of those individuals who was physically incapable of enduring a lie. Her body could not tolerate the tension. She could painfully see her mother contemplating her own demise; even planning it by the abuse she knowingly heaped upon her own body. Laura's psyche grew obstinate. It began to devour all the familiar objects around her. The refrigerator lost its innocence and began to take the form of a coffin. Objects lost their dimensionality, and the room, itself, began to sway. She ran up the stairs in a panic, and threw herself upon the bed. Downstairs, she could still hear the television and the accompanying and awful howling silence. Emotionally exhausted, Laura fell asleep. In her troubled state, she dreamt. The house caught fire. She was trapped in her room as the flames leaped and licked at her. She sat there waiting for the flames to consume her. Suddenly, the house cracked open like an egg, and she took wing and flew into the tranquil night. From a safe and lofty position high in the sky, she looked down upon the place her house had occupied and saw only charred and twisted ruins. Awakened by this dream, Laura felt a strange and inexplicable relief in place of the terror she imagined.

A low but firm knock at her door disturbed her revelry. "Come in," she said quietly. She felt the presence of her father; she fully understood his concern for her well-being.

Her father entered cautiously. He was a large man, but in spite of his size, he always appeared subdued, even obsequious, in the presence of his daughter. "Laura, when you didn't come down for dinner, I got worried. Is anything the matter?"

Laura looked silently into her father's eyes. That prolonged intensity made him feel decidedly uncomfortable. She knew that she could not safely confide in him. As a little girl, she depended upon this towering man for her safety and protection. However, as she grew up, adoration was soon replaced by a growing mistrust, for she never saw his true nature. Intuitively, Laura sensed the presence of a wild uncharted anger that seemed to be festering beneath his eyes. She became afraid of somehow unknowingly triggering its expression. For this reason, she remained very cautious with him, never intimating that she was, in fact, in emotional turmoil. All this, brought her an intense sadness, for she understood just how formidable was the space that separated them.

"Everything is all right," Laura finally answered. "I was very tired and needed to catch up on my sleep. You know, school has been sort of tough lately."

"Yeah, I know. I know you can handle it; I'm so very proud of you. Won't you come down now and join us?"

His mood seemed placid; underneath, however, he felt impotent. The tragic flaw in his nature was his inability to simply and directly express his true feelings. He inevitably became subservient to the ones he loved and endlessly rude and defiant to everyone else.

Together they went downstairs. The cold eye of the television screen maintained its dominance over the woman whose body was impaled upon a big blue cushion. "What am I supposed to do with them?" Laura thought. "I don't know them any more than they know me."

Laura

The three of them sat numbly and absent-mindedly that evening watching television, enraptured by orderly array of electrons hurtling through space at them, impinging upon their retinas, and blurring the distinction between truth and fantasy. Under its influence, all emotions quieted, and a gray passivity, once again, overcame the chaotic tendencies of the family.

The morning barely penetrated Laura's room, for a dark curtain covered the one small window and did not allow daylight to enter. The somber appearance of Laura's space was an accurate reflection of her inner mood. From deep within herself, she felt no expectation or excitement, for each day unfolded predictably like all the rest. The alarm startled her, but she had no desire to uproot herself from hibernation.

In the kitchen, her mother was laboring over omelets. It was her one brief domestic effort of the day. Everyone sat quietly around the table and hurriedly ate breakfast. After both her husband and daughter had been fed and sent on their separate ways, her daily and intimate relationship with alcohol began.

She methodically lowered the shades, closed the curtains, prepared the couch with soft luxuriant pillows, turned on the TV, and readied herself to be swept away by the hidden passions uncorked from the bottle. The world she entered was soft and resilient and freed from pain. Her senses grew languid and more receptive. Her imagination took flight, allowing her to enact the boldest fantasies with imaginary lovers. Only the harsh light of sobriety was vexed with care and responsibility. But in the timeless vertigo of her uprooted mind, there lived only pleasure and its attainment.

Awakening from a Distant Dream

Laura knew nothing of these perceptions, or of the complexity of her mother's inner life. She felt only the pain of her separation from her mother's world which seemed so distant and frightening. The walls that surrounded Laura's life were thick and formidable. She was never more acutely aware of her loneliness then when she left her house in the cool light of morning. As she walked away and turned to look upon that house, she could feel the vacant gray electricity that enshrouded it. This perception made her shiver.

During her walk to school, Laura saw Rachel walking on the other side of the street. They both waved to each other, but remained separated – neither wished to shatter the space of their aloneness. They were neither friends nor enemies but were forced by the rigors of adolescent laws and customs to at least acknowledge each other's existence. Rachel was beginning to blossom into a voluptuous young woman - a course that would help determine the future direction of her existence. A burgeoning self-consciousness together with a highly competitive spirit made Rachel exceedingly caddie especially towards other females. Laura dreaded meeting her. All the banter, the allusions to conquests, the thinly disguised insults exacerbated her insecurities regarding her attractiveness to males and made her inwardly very furious. The anger was further complicated by a secret feeling of intense envy for the way Rachel's body inescapably attracted the interests of the boys. Finally, the fact of her own virginity stuck her like a knife making her feel impotent and alone, she felt like she was a freak of nature. Somewhere in the amazing labyrinth within her, she was chained and a prisoner held fast by the rigid customs and constraints of her age.

Laura

Raymond Valley High School was the root of the mainstream of adolescent social life. Its more rudimentary and vestigial function was that of education. Outside its entrance, students invariably congregated, leaning on their sleek cars and conversing in small exclusive groups; they were submerged in the vivid world of their collective self-indulgence. The majority of students ridiculed and feared the administration and faculty of the school; they reluctantly interrupted their social life to attend classes.

Teachers rarely found a need to establish a rapport with their students and conducted themselves as if they were only remotely connected to what they taught. Mr. Bobrowski was absent-mindedly lecturing about the four chambers of the human heart while the autumn leaves were listlessly drifting across the open field that was framed by the classroom window. Laura, gazing out the window, was peacefully sinking into herself when she was startled by the bell that signaled the end of class.

As she was walking down the wide hallway filled with the noise and chaos that is so effectively propagated by adolescents, Paul ambled towards her. He was awkward and unsure of himself, barely coexisting with the great spurts of energy and growth that were inundating his body. He was wildly attracted to Laura and had tried on numerous occasions to date her. Each time, she had shown no interest. He had a strong ego and an almost incessant manner. He would not take no for an answer. "Hey, Laura," he said, "would you like to see a movie with me this Saturday?" No amount of ardor or enthusiasm could change her feelings towards him. As a matter of fact, the more he pursued her, the less interested she became.

Awakening from a Distant Dream

"Look Paul, I've tried not to hurt your feelings, but how many times are you going to ask me out before you understand that I am just not interested. It has nothing to do with you, really. But please, leave me alone!" Paul looked at her, and said nothing. He walked slowly away feeling terribly hurt and embarrassed. They were both too young to understand the impetus for their own feelings; all they could go by was the power of impulse and intuition.

Generally bludgeoned by the mediocrity of the day, Laura looked forward to the hour she spent in the gymnasium. The breathless activity of her body, which seemed to follow its own innate good sense paying little attention to her preoccupied mind, the manipulations she could put it through with the sweat pouring from her, all these manifestations of herself produced a palpable sense of joy. So taken with such an unbridled sense of herself, Laura paid little attention to Ms. Edna White, her physical education teacher. Edna was a demanding, shrieking woman looking somewhat preposterous in her white briefs. She based her demeanor on the assumption that her students were entirely incapable of making decisions apart from her. Edna was one of those insufferable pedants that so permeated her profession. Many of the more sensitive and timid students would leave her class each day literally trembling with apprehension. It was Laura's good feeling about her own body that made her immune to the ranting of this enraged woman.

During her daily shower in the girl's locker room, Laura's eyes rested on all the youthful female bodies around her. All the exquisite variations on the form of breasts, hips and thighs flooded her senses leaving her strangely aroused. The internal excitement that this generated frightened her. It left her feeling anxious and self-conscious. At such moments, Laura found herself reticent and slightly ashamed. Her classmates were put off by this behavior and reacted by openly chiding and ridiculing her, for they mistook this behavior for snobbery.

Laura

The classes droned on with the same hollow intensity. Day after day, the teachers repeated themselves with the same insipid questions, the same conclusions invariably drawn. Laura's consciousness usually pressed itself against the window, waiting for something extraordinary to happen. Inwardly, she mocked her female classmates. She mocked their passivity. She mocked their opinions of themselves. Laura had no longing to be a cheerleader or to sleep with Mike Farenza the star center for the school basketball team rumored to have the biggest cock in the school. She seemed to have no real loyalty or allegiance to any one person or idea. This troubled her for it seemed to be evidence that something was terribly wrong with her.

During such moments of profound self-doubt, Laura would often seek out her friend Gail. Gail shared many of her innermost feelings. Gail, however, was easy going and self-assured - qualities that were reflected in the way she carried herself. Her life was neatly organized around a surprisingly clear and rational mind. Laura felt safe around Gail. Part of this affinity resided with the fact that Gail was plain looking and did not pose a threat to her own uncertainty about her attractiveness.

They would often meet after class and hang around the school yard. "Gail," Laura said as they were both opposite each other on the seesaw, "did I tell you what happened with Paul?"

"No, what," Gail asked; she suddenly became very attentive.

"Well that jerk asked me out again, can you believe that?"

"Oh I don't know, I think he's kinda cute."

"C'mon Gail, I told you about him. He's just horny. He puts the make on a lot of girls. He doesn't care about me."

"Yeah, I suppose you're right. But at least you get asked out."

Awakening from a Distant Dream

"Would you go out with him?" Laura asked her friend.

"I don't know, maybe."

At first, Laura was irritated by the honesty of this response, but then looking at the mischievous expression in Gail's eyes, they both burst out laughing.

"Seriously," Laura continued, "the guy gives me the creeps. He's just so relentless. He doesn't understand no. I really wonder about him sometimes."

"I know what you mean. Some boys are like that. Maybe they just don't like themselves enough. They think that if they don't insist, they'll never get a date. You know, come to think of it, I often feel that way myself."

"You're funny. You're attractive. I don't know why you don't understand that."

"Attractive, do you think so?"

"Of course I do, and you're such a sweet person. Any guy would be lucky to have you."

"Honestly?"

"Yes, I'm not kidding."

"Laura thanks; that's nice to hear."

As friends, they offered different qualities to each other that neither possessed individually. Although Laura was not a terribly rational human being, she had a magnificent intuitive sense. Their individual talents and shortcomings compensated each other when they were together. At such times, they were relieved of the burden of aloneness that so occupied their lives.

They loved each other, but their bodies were both adolescent and naive. Urgent needs that existed within them remained dormant and unspoken. This left both Laura and Gail feeling unfinished. There were things that they were incapable of doing for each other. This realization was a truth that they were not prepared to address at this time in their lives.

Enter Change with a Vengeance

The fall had finally succumbed to the inexorable arrival of winter. The sun was barely glowing behind its shroud of dark clouds and by late afternoon the winds began to stir. Laura's steps quickened as she left the school grounds. Darkness was already ending the scant hours of winter daylight. Winter was having an exaggerating and amplifying effect upon Laura's generally depressed state of mind. Her mood grew progressively more somber and introspective as the winter wore on. It was for this reason that Laura did not notice that she was being followed.

Paul had never forgiven Laura for shunning him. Her abrupt refusal to go out with him had somehow helped bring to his consciousness a deep and implacable rage. Fate had burdened his innocent soul with the prospect of being an unwanted child caught within the whirlwind of his parent's fiery disillusionment with one another. His mother constantly rebuffed his physical advances to her when he was but a tiny and vulnerable infant. His entire nervous system, as a consequence, ached with an insatiable longing to be held and to be loved, without question.

Laura could not know this, nor, most ironically, could Paul. Her rude dismissal of his intentions drove him back into that emotional void he had felt as a child. The pain was unbearable. His thoughts were wild with both rage and excitement as he followed her home.

He could not accept the idea of yet another rejection. His feelings of love and the irrepressible biology of his hormones that seemed to permeate all his tissues and color his perceptions lived beneath the shadow of his dark and brooding soul. He had come to hate and despise her. He was determined to get even and satisfy himself at the same time. He was shaping his inner self to pursue a life's course that would be filled with folly and regret. He would show her. He would show them all. When he was sure that they were alone, he acted.

Laura was startled as she felt a cold hand over her mouth. He spun her around and yelled, "You bitch! Do you really think you can treat me like a piece of shit? I'm gonna show you."

Before Laura could respond, she was thrown to the hard ground. He leapt upon her and his hands fumbled beneath her dress.

"Paul, please don't," she protested.

At first her body remained rigid and unyielding, but Paul's strength was beginning to overwhelm her. She felt herself grow numb.

In spite of the fact that she was filled with panic, some aspect of her being remained amazingly composed and looked upon the situation with remarkable objectivity. She watched as Paul's face was transformed by the immense fire that seemed to explode from the tempest within him. She reached the point where she believed her fate was already determined and that she possessed no power to avert what now seemed inevitable.

Not far from where this horrid scene was progressing, a lone figure was walking along Wadsworth Avenue. He had a hard and muscular body and walked with a jaunty stride. As he moved, a silent marvelous dance unfolded as if blossoming instantaneously from his sinews. He possessed a youthful exuberance and felt perfectly invincible – a quality of mind that is particularly prevalent in young males. He was direct and decisive in his actions, yet his eyes revealed a softness that suggested a hidden vulnerability.

He was busy running errands. He was a creature of the night, loved the darkness and thrived in its ambiguity. He felt safe and powerful in its embrace. He was a true child of the streets

Enter Change with a Vengeance

As he turned the corner, he happened upon Laura and her attacker. He reacted instinctively. Paul was far too aroused to sense his presence.

He wrapped his arm around Paul's neck, dislodged him from Laura and threw him vehemently to the ground. He stood menacingly over Paul's figure while he asked Laura, "Are you all right?" Laura was far too stunned to respond at first.

Paul looked up at the stranger and realized that he had lost. He felt frightened and, as his ordinary senses returned to him, he began to feel terribly ashamed. Laura's benefactor looked directly at Paul and immediately understood his state of mind.

"Get the hell out of here you son of a bitch! If you touch or threaten this girl ever again you'll be dead meat, you understand?"

Paul nodded as he stood up.

"Beat it!" Danny yelled.

Paul left with a great sinking feeling vividly represented on his face. Some part of his soul died that evening, and a bitter callousness took its place. He became the mere shadow of a person and eventually dropped out of school. He would eventually become a part of that silent brooding army of humans truly lost in the world

Her rescuer extended his hand towards Laura, "Are you okay?"

She gratefully accepted his offer and got up on two very shaky legs. She looked at him with the deepest admiration, "If it wasn't for you, well, I don't even want to think about it."

"Don't think about all that now. Where were you going? Do you want me to walk with you?"

"I was on my way home. But, there is no way I'm going there now."

"How come?" he asked.

Awakening from a Distant Dream

"My parents would never understand. I could never tell them. My father would probably blame me. I can't go there and pretend that nothing ever happened, especially right now."

"Then where will you go?"

"I don't know."

"Then come home with me."

She was startled by his directness and regarded him suspiciously, but when she looked into his eyes, she found kindness there. This left her feeling somewhat confused. "I can't do that; you've done enough already. Besides, I don't even know you."

"Don't be dumb; you can't stay out in the street. Look, you don't need to worry; I'm not going to hit on you." As an afterthought, he said, "My name is Danny, what's yours?"

"Laura," she answered simply.

She was taken aback by his honesty. "I do appreciate what you've done, and I would like to trust you, but right now it's hard. But you're right; I can't really stay on the street."

"Good," he said, "stay with me as long as you like. If you just want to come by for a few hours until you get yourself together well that's okay. Who was that bastard, anyway? Did you know him?"

"Oh him, his name is Paul, just a boy from school. I don't know what got into him. He just wouldn't take no for an answer."

"Oh yeah, I know the type."

"Right now, I feel like I could kill him for what he tried to do to me."

"Sure, I could have killed him myself!" Danny said with arrogant self-assurance.

Enter Change with a Vengeance

Laura felt relieved and remarkably grateful. She felt that she had been saved from the abyss of a devastating experience. However, she was now acutely aware of her own vulnerability as a woman and had grown suspicious of men.

Danny tried to be honest and forthright, but, in fact, he found Laura very attractive. His intentions were never quite honorable; although, he had never been more sincere. At the moment, he felt quite proud of himself for his chivalry and enjoyed the idea that he had rescued Laura from a very bad situation.

He watched her with great interest. He found her to be unlike any woman that he knew. The girls he knew were all too willing to give themselves up to his own personal desires and whims and had very little to say about themselves or what motivated them. It was as if they had no real inner life of their own. The ease of his conquests made them not conquests at all. He was bored. Life had become too predictable. In this way, it almost seemed that Laura had been sent to him to rescue him from his own state of mind. He envisioned possibilities for the future that he could not have anticipated. The incessant void that held dominion over his life was fractured at least for the moment.

Danny had a studio apartment. The front room served as both a living room, and kitchen and the bedroom was in the back. The walls were adorned with posters of almost life-sized sports figures. Laura sat on the couch as Danny attempted to cook dinner. She watched with great interest as he cooked a traditional Italian pasta dish. It was immediately obvious to her that he was inexperienced in this regard and was touched by his desire to please her. She was impressed by how suddenly her life had been changed as a result of one singular event. Laura often viewed her life as if she was an interested onlooker. She did not know whether this was a gift or a curse.

Awakening from a Distant Dream

At first they both felt awkward over dinner. A strange set of circumstances had thrown them together and they knew very little of each other. Finally, Danny spoke to her.

"Laura, you having trouble with your folks?"

Laura was a little startled by this question. "What do you mean?" she asked somewhat defensively.

"Well, you didn't want to go home. You mentioned something about your Dad. Does he beat you?"

"No, he never hit me. I just know he couldn't handle it. He would probably do something drastic. There was no way I could go home and pretend that nothing was wrong. I'm not a good liar. You know what I mean?"

"I guess so. What about your Mom?"

"Oh, her. She's in her own world most of the time. She lies around the house with most of the lights off watching television and she's usually drunk. The funny thing is that she really thinks she's fooling me, when it's so obvious that she's been hitting the bottle. When I come home from school, she's so out of it; she hardly knows that I'm alive." As Laura expressed these feelings, she let her personal demons out and began to sob.

Danny tried his best to comfort her. "That's all right; I know what it's like to have shitty parents. I was abandoned by both of mine. I don't even know where my Dad is. I just try not to think about them. You can't let them take over your life." Danny was not used to speaking so openly about himself; it was very painful. In spite of that, he felt that the burden he carried in the depth of his being grow measurably lighter.

After Laura calmed herself, she said, "Thank you for listening to me."

"Don't mention it. You wanta watch some TV?"

Enter Change with a Vengeance

"No thanks. I'm tired of watching that thing. That's all my mother does all day long. That's what the family does with the time we have together. Besides, I'm really exhausted. Would you mind if I crashed here tonight?"

"No not at all," he quickly answered, barely disguising the enthusiasm he felt. "You can sleep in my bed tonight; I'll sleep on the couch."

"I can't let you do that," she responded, "it's your place."

He feigned an imperious expression, "Look, don't argue, okay. You've been through a lot. I won't have it any other way!"

"All right, Danny," she replied. "Thank you." As Laura was getting ready for bed, she realized what a strange turn her life had taken. She never would have imagined that she would be spending the night in a stranger's bed. She was becoming more acutely aware of her own sexuality. On account of the momentous events that just transpired, Laura recognized the depths of her sexual inexperience. This realization left her feeling terribly uneasy. In spite of this, she felt so emotionally and physically exhausted that sleep gradually overtook her

As Danny was lying awake on the couch, the thought of Laura sleeping on his bed aroused him. Moreover, he thought about what his friends would say if they found out that he had a girl over and didn't "give it" to her. He could hear their scorn and ridicule. He could see that they never would understand. To Danny, his reputation was his lifeblood.

Awakening from a Distant Dream

He made a momentous decision and got up off the couch and walked towards the bedroom. He quietly went inside and got under the covers beside her. He snuggled up to her, wrapped his arm around her and kissed her tenderly on the shoulder. Her sleeping body responded. This encouraged him to take further liberties with her. His left hand moved up her abdomen and cupped her breast.

The sensation startled Laura and she quickly sat up. "What are you doing?" His arm was still around her and he forced her onto her back.

"I want you baby!" he said as he straddled her.

"No, no," she implored, "please don't." He put his hand over her mouth and was going to penetrate her. But, when he looked at her and saw the fright and despair in her eyes, his penis just wilted. He sighed deeply and fell away from her.

She was horrified and angry, terribly angry. "You son of a bitch," she yelled, "This is what you call protection. You were going to take advantage of me. You just figured you could come in here and try to do the same thing to me that Paul wanted to do. You didn't give one minute's thought to my feelings. I was really dumb to think I could trust you, you bastard!" Her entire body was filled with rage. As she was screaming, she couldn't believe that she was saying these things. It had never occurred to her to express her angry so freely before - it felt liberating. She never thought that she had the right. The fact that she was nearly violated twice in a single day by two different men was enough to release her long held inhibitions. "I was sleeping and you were going to force yourself on me. What kind of person are you?" As she said this, she hurriedly leapt out of bed and put her clothes on.

Enter Change with a Vengeance

Danny looked at her and something happened inside of him. For the first time, the idea of a woman took on an entirely new meaning. It was as if even with all his so-called sexual expertise he was still a virgin, for he had immunized himself against the longings of his own heart. No woman had ever challenged his authority like that. He fell in love with this person who he had first perceived as a weak and vulnerable girl. Part of this attraction may have been due to the fact that she stood up to him and now seemed unattainable. It was her passion that intrigued him. He did not want her to leave, especially feeling as she did. He really did care for her.

"Wait," he said as Laura was quickly gathering up her things to go.

"What!" she answered ferociously but still willing to listen to an explanation.

"You're right, I'm sorry. Just the idea of a girl in my bed made me horny."

"Oh, so that means that gives you the right to jump on me. What's with that anyway? Because you're horny, does that mean I'm supposed to fix it? I'm here to help you get your rocks off!"

Danny was dumbfounded; he had no legitimate answer to that question. He had never been challenged in this way; he chose to be silent.

Laura took that silence to be a vindication. She was still propelled by her new found power - discovered in the strangest of circumstances. Also, she realized as she looked at this youthful well-structured male, that she was madly attracted to him. This feeling abated her anger and dulled the sharpness of her tone.

Danny saw that she had not left. "Look," he said, "I know you're mad, but there is really nowhere for you to go tonight. Please, go back to bed. I'll leave you alone. Tomorrow you can do what you want. Maybe we can still talk; maybe we can still be friends. Okay?" he implored.

Awakening from a Distant Dream

She looked carefully at him. "Okay, but you'll have to leave right now so that I can get back to sleep."

After he had gone, Laura paid attention to all the details of the space she was in. She could not help but see the two large posters of women in various states of undress, the clothes chaotically strewn about the room and the dresser with the cracked mirror. She found all of this unsettling. She felt that the chaos of Danny's life and emotions was reflected in the space he occupied. The fact that he had just tried to take advantage of her in spite of the state of her mind was inescapable. These were all warning signs of what she might have to deal with if she really got involved with him. In spite of this, she chose to stay the night. Possibly, these considerations were all too much for her to contend with after all that she had just been through. It was not long before she finally went to sleep; although, it was restless and fitful. She was periodically awakened by dreams whose contents she was unable to remember.

It is not uncommon for the young to take extraordinary risks even when their safety is in jeopardy. Laura, as a naive and callow woman, hungered for experience and may have felt that kind of foolish invincibility that is so common among the young.

When she awoke the next morning, she was at first startled to find herself in a strange room. She quickly remembered how she got there and the inescapable fact that she was almost raped not once but twice by two different men. Fear and uncertainty began to take hold of her. She drew the covers more tightly around herself and remained in bed for quite some time. Finally she left the room with some trepidation, and found breakfast waiting for her. Danny gestured to the table. "Would you like some coffee," he asked.

She looked at him intently trying to gauge his feelings. "Yes, yes thank you," she answered.

Enter Change with a Vengeance

Danny recognized the fear in Laura's eyes. Fear was a creature that he lived with and learned to respect and nurture. He was not quite sure what he felt for her, but was sure that he had never felt this way about another human being. "Did you sleep well?" he asked.

"Yes I did," she said. By her expression, Danny knew it was not true. Laura was not very good at disguising her feelings. She wore her heart about her like an amulet. She had never learned the ability to project a mood outwardly towards the world that was contrary to what was within. This kind of deception can be an important skill in the toolkit of survival.

"About last night," Danny began awkwardly, "I'm sorry. I've never met anyone quite like you. I don't usually hang out with girls like you."

Laura was not quite sure what he meant. Nonetheless, she decided to let it pass. "Well, let me put it this way, I'm not sure about you and after yesterday I am not sure about my feelings towards men in general. At least you were good enough to let me sleep."

After this initial awkwardness, they both tried to be civil to each other.

As they sat in silence at the table eating breakfast, Laura could not help realizing that she felt somewhat aroused in his presence. She had so little experience regarding her own sexuality that she did not know how to navigate within this realm. To distract herself, she directed her attention towards conversation.

"Danny," she began, "tell me about yourself."

"Me, well, I don't know what to tell you!"

"First off, what is your full name? All I know is that you're Danny."

"I'm Danny Ferguson."

Laura looked at him expectantly, patiently waiting for him to tell her more. But he remained reticent. This made Laura impatient.

Awakening from a Distant Dream

"Come on Danny; how about some details. Do you go to school? What about your family? I want to know more."

"School, that's easy to answer; I went to the same school you're probably going to right now. Man, I hated that place. I remember some days I was so bored that I felt like I could kill somebody. I couldn't wait to get out of there. But I did a really dumb thing; I dropped out."

"What about your family? You told me a little about your Dad."

"Me and my Mom were living in a homeless shelter at the time. She was usually so wasted that she didn't care about what I was doing; I rarely saw her anyway."

"Where is your Mom now?" Laura asked.

"She died. One morning she simply didn't wake up."

"Oh how awful! I'm so sorry; that must have been painful for you."

"No, not really. As a matter of fact, I felt relieved. I hated her. The way she treated me. When she got into her drunken rages she would hit me and curse me and make me feel like shit." As Danny spoke, he began to grow agitated. This scared Laura, yet she continued.

"How awful! What about your Dad?"

Danny's state of mind grew more disturbed. His face grew tight, and she could see his jaw go rigid. He tried to calm himself, "He left us years ago," he finally answered.

"I'm sorry," she said. They both became quiet. She could see that it was painful for him and knew that she needed to change the subject. "This is a nice place; it must be expensive. How can you afford it?" she asked.

"I hustle."

"Hustle?"

"Yeah, you know; I get people what they need."

"What do you mean?"

Enter Change with a Vengeance

"You can't be that naive. You know - women, drugs, false IDs, guns, stuff like that."

Laura's face suddenly turned ashen. Her disposition towards Danny changed from one of friendly interest into one of suspicion and mistrust. It suddenly reminded her of his behavior the night before. Her silence was profound; her features grew immobile. This revelation about Danny now resided incongruously within her mind next to the inchoate feelings of desire for him.

"What's the matter; you don't like that do you? You people are all the same; you have this kind of moral superiority that you parade around whenever it suits you."

"I don't know what you're talking about!" she responded. "I didn't say anything."

"Yeah, right, c'mon I could see it in your face. You find it all so horrible and disgusting, right! But it's okay for the people who I do business with to live in shit up to their eyeballs. Isn't it?"

Laura could not answer, for she realized that he had a point, and it was too profound a criticism for her to immediately admit to. He was still angry and Laura found the power of that anger strangely attractive, for it gave Danny dimension in her eyes. She could see that beneath his tough exterior, he was lonely, afraid and vulnerable. Once she could relax her guard, she could feel her body being drawn towards his. She felt the power and magnetism of his being inundate her.

He continued, "Laura you need to understand that this is my life, and I have no problems about what I do. If you do, then you should not stay here." He purposefully placed a lot of emphasis on this last statement.

Awakening from a Distant Dream

He could see that her feelings for him were changing right before his eyes. He was amazed by the transformation and would have never expected it. She was falling for him much as the rain falls with a wild and tumultuous rush in its inexorable descent to earth. His feelings were not quite as exact. He was far too protective of himself and manipulative to expose his inner self to quite that extent. Danny was a creature honed on survival and inured to the rush of adrenalin.

The bed covers were filled with the aroma of their sex and impregnated with the fabric of their desire. Laura was no longer a virgin. She was surprised at how quickly it all happened. In one moment, he was on top of her, and in the next he was spent. His orgasm was explosive and brief. Although her experience with sex was completely new, she felt somewhere within her that what she did feel in the midst of lovemaking was not all that she was capable of. She found this conclusion inexplicable even to herself. Yet when she looked in Danny's eyes, she thought she saw a good man and a gentle human being beneath his tough exterior. She came to the naive and dangerous conclusion that she could somehow redeem him; that she could help change him.

Their bodies were piled up on top of each other like cord wood. Their breaths were heavy but strangely quiet. "Danny," she said as she held his face tenderly in her hands, "I love you."

Danny looked at her and realized that for the first time he really loved another human being. He kissed her with great tenderness, and simply said, "You must stay here with me. I don't want you to go."

Enter Change with a Vengeance

"Yes, I will," she replied. She did not say this without reservation, for she could not help but remember his violent behavior. Implacable circumstances and the urgency of desire, however, often have a way of exerting the final say in human affairs. He again took her in his arms and made love to her. This time she tried to pay closer attention to her feelings as well.

Love is a word so easily spoken, yet its power and meaning can either be deeply profound or hollow and without real substance. Laura and Danny were untried in the ways of love and were driven by that youthful appetite for experience.

A Sense of Loss

Edward Curtis was walking up his front steps. Being a bus driver often can be an unnerving experience. He had a particularly bad day. As he opened the door an unanticipated sense of dread came over him. Ordinarily he suppressed his true feelings, but for some reason this evening they were particularly prevalent. He walked up to Ruth in her usual place on the couch, and kissed her on the forehead. She shifted her gaze from the television to him only for an instant.

"Where is Laura?"

"Up in her room, I think," she answered.

"She's been so quiet and withdrawn lately."

"It's just her age!" Ruth answered showing some irritation at having to be forced to take her attention away from the television and engage in conversation. Showing her annoyance in this way was a useful strategy that accomplished its purpose - shutting off any chance at dialogue.

He went into the bedroom to freshen himself up and change his clothes. His thoughts were random and disconnected. Underlying his state of mind was a feeling of foreboding that would not go away. His mind took him back to a summer day many years ago. It was a vivid remembrance of him and Ruth making love on a beach in Mexico. They were on their honeymoon. He could feel his body being aroused and excited. He could almost feel the hot summer sun on his back. These feelings had long been dormant within him. He remembered how playful they used to be together, how their bodies responded to each other without effort. These recollections sometimes interjected themselves within his mind. Such thoughts were always unnerving and would surely drive him crazy if he persisted in that direction. As an antidote, he learned to send his mind off onto an excursion into the more distant past.

"I tell you the boy is psychic," the wizened old lady said.

"Don't be silly, Emma!" her friend answered. "He's just a boy. Where do you get such crazy thoughts?"

"You may make fun of me, but I know these things. He's like me; he can see into the future. He knows when things are about to happen. He is like me. You'll see."

The other woman, Maria, smiled, but her upper lip twitched ever so slightly. She knew that her son, Edward, was a strange child. She knew that he was not like the other children. This worried her sometimes. Her little boy looked up at his mother with soulful eyes and tugged at her blouse. She looked at him and saw a single tear dance down his cheek.

Edward remembered that day so clearly, but he never quite understood its meaning. This recollection had always remained vivid within his mind. He could not recall the place or, for that matter, the time. It was an insight into his true nature that he failed to take it into account in his own life. It was an essential aspect of his being that had been torn from him as a result of the environment in which he grew up. In his experience, he rarely felt at peace, for there was always some crisis to hurtle, some hurt to endure and some pain to accommodate. Such thoughts were unsettling; he routinely denied their importance.

When he was done dressing, he went downstairs to join his wife. As he walked into the living room, Ruth absentmindedly turned to him, "Your dinner is on the stove." This fleeting sense of recognition was gone almost as quickly as it came. Edward went into the kitchen and ate by himself.

Awakening from a Distant Dream

Later that evening as he was staring into the space directly in front of the television, he thought, "Where is Laura."

"I'm going upstairs to find out if Laura wants to eat," he said to his wife. Moments later he returned, "I thought you said Laura was in her room," exposing the annoyance he felt.

"I thought she was! Don't you go using that tone with me! Am I supposed to know her whereabouts every moment? She's probably off somewhere with her friends. Now don't get excited, all right."

"How could you be so calm!" he stammered. "Your daughter is gone. You don't know where she is and you don't seem to care. You don't seem to care about anything. You just lie there as if nothing has happened. I don't understand you." Ruth looked at him in complete astonishment. She hadn't seen him so angry or so passionate about anything for years.

After saying this and knowing only too well that Ruth would not respond to him, he got up and left her alone as she had wanted. Whatever residual feelings that remained with her, were decapitated by the profound influence of alcohol that permeated every tissue of her body and numbed her senses. Ruth was no longer of this world, and no longer capable of living in it. She was waiting for death to come and deliver her finally from it all. Her decline was not sudden. It had taken many years of the gradual deterioration of her spirit to reach her current state of existence. There was no one that could truly be blamed for this. Life wore her down; she did not possess sufficient resilience to weather life's disappointments. Ruth ultimately chose drink as her most intimate companion.

It was during such moments that Edward felt rage expand into his chest like a hot balloon. He wanted to go up to Ruth pick up her off the couch and shake her until she responded. He wanted to drag her into the present. He longed for the intimacy they once had. Within his darkest fantasies, he wanted to kill her then himself, but would not for Laura's sake. He loved his daughter with all the love that his heart was capable of. He worried about her constantly. He loved Ruth as well but it was love put in a deep freeze. All he could do was remember the love and affection he was once able to express to her. But now, the cavern was too deep, the fortress too impregnable to be breached by mere desire or hunger. Even the hunger had died, leaving only the trappings of a vague familiarity and the undeniable history of their life together.

On Becoming a Woman

Laura looked at her life and recognized that it had suddenly and irrevocably changed. She was no longer going to school; she was no longer living at home and now she was living with a man to whom she felt devoted; because, he had quite literally saved her life. The singular price she paid for this transformation was that she was no longer living for herself, but in many ways was living for another person.

She found that her days were quickly consumed with the tasks of maintaining a home. She swept and dusted and mopped and washed the dishes and cooked the meals. Most of her energy was spent catering to and cleaning up after Danny. How she had come to this place, she was not sure.

Danny, for his part, welcomed and encouraged this behavior. It fit precisely into the image he had of what a relationship with a woman should be. He had grown to expect that his physical needs would be regularly met. In a matter of months, Laura had found herself being taken for granted. This did not occur to her on an emotional level at first. The frustration was escalating within her psyche. It was only through the natural course and evolution of events that these feelings would be suddenly catapulted to the surface.

They had fallen into the conventional habits of a married couple. With married couples, however, the progression is a prolonged one, preceded by years of romantic involvement that gradually evolves into entrenched roles dictated by both culture and circumstance. For Danny and Laura, this progression was tremendously accelerated possibly because they were unsure of each other and somewhat distrustful. Laura occupied herself with household chores as a way of distracting herself from the fact that she had no goals that were truly her own. Not far beneath the surface, she was frustrated and untested.

Ironically, however, she found that she had gone from the house of her parents where she exerted very little influence if any, to a house where she, likewise, had very little impact, and in which she was taking care of a man in a relationship that left her feeling terribly ambivalent. Her own life, as of yet, had not established itself in the world. She had no real sense of herself as an autonomous human being. In a very essential way, this was proving to be very unsatisfactory state of existence. On some level of awareness, change was inevitable, for she was being readied for an exploration of her true nature.

Danny usually left home in the early afternoon, and never revealed his whereabouts to Laura. He also returned whenever he pleased. His life and the patterns of his existence remained essentially unchanged since Laura had moved in with him. His aggressive behavior towards the world had always protected him from his underlying feelings of desperation and despair, or so he thought. He did not trust in anyone or anything. His past and the pain he had endured growing up had convinced him that he was not worthy of love. This self-image was so deeply embedded in his psyche that his outward behavior modeled this conception.

On this particular morning as Danny was leaving, Laura absentmindedly asked, "When will you be home?"

"Look, baby," Danny responded, "how many times do I have to tell you that you don't need to know that, and I have no idea myself when I will be home. So, get out of my face! Got it?"

"All right," Laura answered. She had asked that question on a number of occasions. She always got essentially the same response.

Awakening from a Distant Dream

That night, Danny came home about 11:30 with four of his neighborhood friends. They were obviously all high on waves of narcotic euphoria. Laura was asleep in the bedroom; she had given up waiting for him. He yelled at the top of his voice, "Hey baby, I'm home. I brought some friends with me."

Laura was startled out of bed and quickly put on a robe before she ventured out into the living room. She was immediately confronted by a house full of strangers who seemed to show no respect for her person or her privacy. They were so unaffected by Laura's presence that she felt nearly invisible. They were sprawled out all over the living room. They were all apparently dosed up with a wide variety of brain-altering chemicals and worst of all they wreaked. She looked at Danny with anger glaring in her eyes and a feeling of disgust promenading in her belly.

He paid her no mind. "Honey, could you get us some beer?" he asked. Despite the dark feelings that enshrouded her, she obeyed. At that moment, she despised her passivity that she mistakenly took for cowardice.

The night wore on like a grade B movie. She abandoned herself to a chair in the corner of the room, and noticed with alarm the increasing state of chaos knowing full well that it would be her task to make it all right when everyone had gone home. This made her furious. She was so filled with disgust that she decided to busy herself in the kitchen.

By two o'clock in the morning, all the guests left except for Rodney who was one of Danny's closest friends. Rodney was totally wasted on a cornucopia of stimulants, narcotics and alcohol. His eyes were glazed and his general expression was one of advanced stupor. He had thrown up while on the couch and had fallen asleep in his own excrement.

Sometime later Danny called out, "Laura let's go to bed." When she didn't answer he said, "Laura where the fuck are you?"

On Becoming a Woman

Laura, reluctantly came out into the living room. "Yeah," she said, "what do you want?"

"Let's go to bed," with the suggestion in his voice that his aim was not sleep.

"What about him!" Laura demanded, pointing to Rodney.

"He can sleep it off on the couch."

"Bullshit," she said, walking over to the couch and violently shaking the sleeping form. "Get the hell up," she shouted, "and get out of here."

Danny was totally taken aback by Laura's behavior. He had never seen her act quite like this. "Hey," he yelled, "what are you doing?"

"Isn't it obvious! I want this guy out."

Rodney was completely unresponsive to her urging, which made her more and more desperate. Danny walked behind her, grabbed her by the arm and pulled her towards him. "Leave him alone; what's gotten into you, anyway!"

She looked at him intently. Her eyes were aflame. "I'm tired of this. You ignore me most of the time unless you want something from me. You don't give a damn about me. All I seem to do is pick up after you. You're such a slob, I can't believe it.

"And sex, all you seem to want is sex. Most of the time, you don't seem to care if I'm satisfied or not. I'm beginning to despise you."

In the midst of her anger, Laura was quite surprised by her own boldness and the sheer power of her emotions. She was not quite sure where this came from; it seemed so completely out of character. But, she did know that it felt good to unleash her feelings in this way. She was, in fact, emboldened by how relieved this release of accumulated frustrations made her feel.

Awakening from a Distant Dream

Danny stood there for long moments overwhelmed by her unexpected anger. He was astonished at this radical transformation in her behavior. He could not comprehend what had motivated her to suddenly behave in this way. He had grown entirely dependent upon her timidity and apparent submissiveness. This feeling of surprise and shock was soon supplanted by the feeling that he had been betrayed. At that moment, he stood at an emotional crossroads. He could have calmed himself and listened to what she was trying to tell him, or he could allow his raw emotions to once again dictate his behavior. He chose to take the route that was most familiar to him. "Look bitch," he screamed, "no woman is gonna talk to me like that. Shut your mouth."

"Don't tell me to shut up. You bring home your filthy friends carrying who knows what kind of disease expecting me to cater to them as well as you. Give me a break! I won't stand for it any longer."

Suddenly, Laura felt Danny's fist crash against her jaw and she fell backwards striking her head against the arm of the couch. Before she could fully regain her senses, Danny was sprawled on top of her. He grabbed the top of her robe and pulled it down tearing it in the process. He then fumbled with his zipper. She looked up still in a daze to see what was obviously transpiring. "Please," she screamed, "Danny don't. Please!"

He smashed her across the face with his opened hand, and as she lay there in a semi-conscious state, he pulled down her panties and penetrated her. Even though she was barely aware and completely unresponsive, he thrust into her, violating and undermining whatever semblance of intimacy existed between them. He was determined to kill whatever spark of love remained. When he was done, he got up and looked down at the pathetic figure sprawled before him on the floor. He was so filled with remorse and self-loathing that he quickly transposed his feelings to hatred for his victim. His emotions were cold and unforgiving. "Son of a bitch," he said under his breath and left the apartment.

In spite of herself, Laura fell asleep from exhaustion right there in the same spot where she had been violated. When she finally did wake up a few hours later, the vivid reality of that rape came back to her. She was so full of rage that she jumped up and turned around to see Rodney on the couch. It was upon him that she unleashed all her fury. She grabbed him by his hair and pulled so forcefully that a giant wad of hair was left in her clenched fist. Rodney was so out of it that he barely stirred. She then grabbed him by his shirt and pulled him with all the remaining strength available to her; until, he fell off the couch. She went to the kitchen to get a giant carving knife, stood over his body kicking him savagely until he awoke.

"What the fuck," he said in amazement. As he eyes began to focus, he saw the terrifying image of a woman threatening him with a huge knife. He could tell by her expression that this was no game.

"If you don't get the fuck out of here right now," she said, "I'm gonna push this blade right into your chest."

"Okay, okay," he answered keeping his hands raised as a gesture of surrender and supplication. In a few moments, all traces of his presence were gone.

Laura dropped the knife, sat down on the couch and began to sob. It was a grief that came from the very core of her being. "That bastard!" she thought, "saved me from being raped only to take me for himself. What a fool I am to trust. Never again! Never again!" On further reflection, she thought, " I shouldn't be surprised; I've known all along what he was capable of. I just thought he loved me – what a fool!" She repeated this over and over like a mantra.

She hurriedly packed all her belongings. She was determined to leave before she'd have to see Danny, for she knew what he was capable of doing to her. She was determined to take better care of herself in the future.

Awakening from a Distant Dream

The trauma of that experience would haunt her for years. However, as a result, she came face to face with the formidable and determined side of her own nature, which would eventually prove to be a good thing.

Even though Danny was filled with a fury that had, like so many times before, fueled his own brutality, his own inner intelligence knew that he had wronged Laura in a way that was irreparable. He was lost in a cycle of behavior that he did not know how to stop; a pattern that he seemed powerless to control. He had never lived in an environment created by loving relationships. He remembered only too vividly his father's own ominous bearing and heavy hands as they often fell upon him as a young boy. He was only too familiar with his own feelings of bitterness, frustration and anger. Those were precisely the feelings that made him feel alive and truly in control of his own destiny. In fact, he did not know how to respond to the love, kindness and generosity of others; to him, they seemed to be alien emotions.

Danny had surrounded himself with an impenetrable wall that others could only enter at their own risk. Ironically, Laura was the only person that he had allowed to approach as closely as she did. She did so, however, at her own peril. Now, he found himself alone once again. Tragically, he buried this inner voice for it was far too painful for him to listen to. The street and the chaos it engendered called to him once again and he responded.

Teacher

As she was leaving Danny's apartment, she was struck by the enormity of the task in front of her. "Now what do I do?" she asked herself. She had some savings that she accumulated from working summer jobs. She was surprised by how much money she had actually saved, and planned to make it last as long as possible. She withdrew everything from her account and opened up a new account at a different bank. This simple act was symbolic of the fact that she was determined to take her own life in hand. Next, she searched the classified ads for a place to live. She felt a deep sense of urgency, and, therefore, made a whole series of momentous decisions. She decided to pay very close attention to her own particular needs and was determined to never again be forced to make bad decisions based purely on what others might expect from her.

She also decided to return to school and get her diploma with an eye towards a profession. At the moment, she had not the faintest idea about what direction her life might take, but she vowed to herself that she would find out. She also hoped to eventually reconcile with her parents, but only after she had established her own independence. This was the most difficult goal for her to envision, since the emotional gulf between them was so enormous.

Luckily, she managed to find a small studio apartment within walking distance of her school. It was ideally suited to meet her needs, and it was something she could afford. She then re-enrolled in school. It was only after these necessary details were worked out that Laura allowed herself to feel the full power of the emotions of her recent experience. The fury that was locked away in her heart needed no fuel to be reignited. The hatred, disgust and loathing she felt were not only projected towards the perpetrator of the terrible deed, but to all men. She came to believe that they were all cold and brutal; that women were cursed by their biology and that life was best endured alone. These were certainly dark and heavy ideas for such a young person to take on. Experience, however, has a way of casting deep shadows over the mind's illustrious eye. She considered having Danny charged with rape. But, she concluded that to pursue such a course would be far too costly and painful; she wanted to move past this experience as quickly as possible.

The first day of her return to the classroom was a strange one. She found herself having to try to adapt to an environment that she had completely outgrown, yet it afforded a kind of protection for her, and gave her life some semblance of stability no matter how illusory.

Most of her acquaintances had either graduated, quit school or moved on to college. She felt not unlike an interloper. Her movements and mannerisms reflected the feeling of being a pariah in her own school. Everyone who dealt with her seemed to keep their distance, or so she thought. In fact, other students did not know how to interact with her. She no longer shared any of the concerns or predilections of her peers.

Her focus was predominantly within herself. She longed to fathom the depths of her own nature, her womanhood, and her feelings. There was no accepted niche in the culture for such pursuits, especially not high school where peer pressure exerts enormous influence on adolescent thinking. Laura was no longer subject to these influences.

The teachers themselves offered no real relief. Most of the energy in the classroom was devoted to maintaining order within the whirlwind and chaos of youth. Teachers were not accustomed to challenge the higher faculties of their charges.

Teacher

Ms. Audrey Wrey, the art teacher, was an exception. She was an airy soul, Aquarian in nature, whose flights of idealism carried her students along with her. She was a sculptress by profession, who taught art, and the enthusiasm she generated among her students often felt threatening to her peers.

Laura had heard of her, and longed to meet her although she herself was intimidated by both art and the world of artists. They seemed to represent a will towards freedom that frightened her. Something inside of her, however, was aware of an inner need that encouraged her to explore that world.

The art class was bright and colorful. This was not due to any difference in design, for the room shared the same bland and cost effective architecture as the rest of the building, but rather to the imagination and creativity of the teacher. The walls were filled with the richly textured art created by her students over the years.

On the first day of class, the students were noisy and disruptive as they waited for the teacher. Audrey always made a late entrance purposefully. She wanted to create an atmosphere of dramatic tension. Laura was sitting in the back already growing skeptical about this teacher's reputation.

The teacher finally entered. She was exquisitely beautiful. The boys in the class - even the ones who knew her - suddenly grew collectively quiet as their lungs emptied of air. She was tall and lithe. Her hair was auburn, full and long. It had an untamed quality about it. Her gate was light and full of self-assurance. Her face was soft and open and her eyes were deep brown. She had a remarkably imposing presence. Most of the girls were instantly jealous; they secretly would like to have killed her. Laura, on the other hand, felt herself strangely attracted to her. This feeling made her uneasy, for she did not understand it.

"Class," she began, "I'm Audrey Wrey and I'll be teaching you art appreciation. But let me tell you right off, don't expect to sit back in this class and just look at pictures. You're going to work your butts off in here. This is a hands-on class. You're going to get your hands dirty, believe me. Art is not easy. It takes a struggle to use the materials at hand and turn them into an expression of your inner self. But once you make it work, it's such a powerful feeling. I can't tell you enough in that regard.

"We'll begin simply by making sketches, simple drawings, looking and talking about other artists' works. But I'll be demanding a lot from you as the year progresses. Just look around you," as she pointed to the walls in the classroom, "these were all done by students most of whom did not regard themselves as artists when they began.

"You see, there is a ridiculous mystique about art. It is not possessed exclusively by the chosen few; it is in all of us. So in my class, you will not play at art or merely observe art, you will do art."

Laura was quite taken by Audrey. She was awed by her beauty and impressed by her intellect. She had never had a teacher quite like her. The rest of school including all the classes, teachers and students seemed insignificant in comparison. Right at that moment, she decided two things. The first was that she would have a personal relationship with her teacher, and secondly that she would work very hard in her class. Art suddenly seemed to appeal to her. It might possibly fulfill some of her deeper needs and help develop her skills of observation and her sensitivity as a person. The more she thought about it, the more she realized that her temperament might very well be suited to be an artist. Her wide swings in mood, the delicate state of her nerves, and the volatility of her

Teacher

emotions were all patent signs of her artistic nature. These thoughts grew on her as the year progressed.

One day while the class was working with the medium of watercolor, Laura was busy sketching the boy who was modeling in the front of the class. As she became engrossed in what she was doing, a part of her deep inner self had a profound revelation. At that singular moment Laura realized that she had found a focus for her life, for she realized that while she was in the midst of creating, the passing of time became essentially irrelevant. She became lost in the midst of her endeavor. Laura understood that it was a discipline that would take years to nurture and develop. It was what she needed; it was what she required. At the end of that class, Laura went up to her teacher.

"Ms. Wrey," she began, "I love this class; I think you're wonderful."

"Thank you, Laura," she replied. "Look, you can call me Audrey; no need to be so formal."

"I think I want to be an artist," she continued.

"Well that is encouraging. I like to hear my students say that. It means that I'm having an effect. I must remind you, the life of an artist is not an easy one. This culture really doesn't support the arts in any real way. As an artist, you'd be constantly worrying about money, for you'll never have enough of it. You'll have periods when you can't seem to create anything. During those times, you'll wonder why you really bothered at all. Don't get me wrong, I'm not trying to discourage you, but you need to know the whole truth not just the romantic aspects.

"But, on the other hand, it's those moments of clarity and pure creativity that make the entire thing worth it. I'd be more than happy to encourage you in any way that I can. Okay. Shall we shake on it?" Audrey extended her hand. Laura noted that when their hands were clasped together, Audrey applied a subtle almost voluptuous

Awakening from a Distant Dream

pressure. Laura was surprised how she found herself responding to this subliminal message.

Each day Laura looked forward to going to Audrey's class, and each day she would find some kind of pretext for staying after class and talking to her. One day after Audrey had introduced the students to sculpture, and they had begun their individual projects, Laura asked her teacher, "Ms. Wrey," Audrey interrupted her, "Please Laura, call me Audrey, I prefer it."

Laura looked at her intently. "Very well, Audrey aren't you a sculptress?"

"I am," she answered.

"Why don't you talk about your own work in class? Why don't you let us see it?"

"I don't know; maybe I think it would be using the students as if they were a captive audience. I don't think that would be very fair, do you?"

"No I guess it wouldn't," Laura replied. "But, I'd still like to see your work?"

"Well now, that's different. You can come over to my place any time."

Laura could not get out of her head this brief conversation with Audrey. She could not forget the way Audrey looked at her. It excited her and frightened her at the same time. Ultimately she dismissed these feelings as trivial and unimportant and probably stemming from her own vivid imagination.

Laura was working on her piece, a clay self-portrait. She was so lost in her own creativity that she did not notice Audrey's presence; until, she felt the soft and warm touch of her hand upon her shoulder. This touch sent a shock wave through her body that she could not ignore. She felt flushed and strangely exhilarated. Audrey bent down and with their faces almost touching said, "Laura, this piece is exquisite. It seems to capture an inner longing. I've been noticing how you work and how you use your hands and the detail that you impart to your work. I think you have the gift. I believe you're ready. Why don't you come by my place tonight about seven o'clock, and we can talk about this some more," at which point she handed Laura a slip of paper with her address and phone number on it.

That evening, she walked over to Audrey's neighborhood that she knew quite well. It was early spring. The sounds of boisterously mating frogs could be heard in the pond across the road. The evening seemed to shimmer in the fading light of day. The air was balmy and felt like a gigantic comforter that wrapped itself around her. The brightest stars were already securing their positions in the night sky. It was the kind of evening the body revels in and remembers its place in the nature of things. She was so lost in these feelings that she almost forgot what she was doing.

She looked at the slip of paper with Audrey's address under the muted glow of a street lamp. Audrey's place was a few houses down the street. As she went up the walk to the front door, she suddenly grew unsettled, for she remembered Audrey's touch and the sweetness of her words.

When Audrey opened the door, she visibly brightened, "Laura, come in. I wasn't sure whether you would come or not. I'm so happy that you did."

Laura came in but her movements could not disguise the tentativeness of her emotions. She stood awkwardly in the middle of the room. Audrey took her jacket.

"Come over here and sit down," Audrey said as she sat on the couch. It was a small couch and when Laura sat down, their bodies were quite close to each other. "Laura you seem so nervous, how come?"

"I've never been to a teacher's house before." She said this as she looked all around her.

Awakening from a Distant Dream

Audrey knew that this was not the complete explanation, but she continued, "So what do you think?"

"Oh it's wonderful. I've never seen so much art in one place. Are all of these your own creations?"

"Oh no, not at all. Besides being an artist, I am also an art collector. I love art of all kinds. The way I see it Laura is that art provides us a snapshot of the soul. It shows how the artist sees his environment, how he relates to it and how he responds to it. That was what you showed me in your sculpture. And that is why I want to know you better and encourage you as much as I can." Audrey purposefully stopped here so that that idea would rest lightly on Laura's mind.

"What did you see in my sculpture?" Laura asked. Her curiosity was fully engaged.

"Well, I saw the character of your person; I saw your vulnerability and I saw your pain."

"Pain!" Laura exclaimed not expecting to be so transparent.

"It was obvious to me that you are in pain. Do you really believe that you can cover it up? Do you want to talk about it? You can trust me."

Suddenly, the simple acknowledgment by someone else that she was in pain was enough for her to drop her defenses. Her face portrayed the tension and the silence seemed unbearable.

"I feel so all alone. I have no one I can really talk to. I have no one that I trust enough to tell what I'm really feeling and thinking. I feel like such a freak sometimes. I've tried to have relationships with men, but I've had such rotten luck. I just don't know anymore. I feel so frustrated, and I don't know what I'm really doing. It seems that I could be an artist, but I just don't know. Sometimes I think that I can't do anything."

Then, she literally came apart and fell into Audrey's arms. This state of being seemed to persist for a long period of time. Audrey comforted her with compassion and

Teacher

warmth. She gently stroked her hair and brushed the tears away from her eyes with her hand. A bond was cemented between them at that moment, whether they had wished it or not.

When Laura finally was calm enough, she raised her head and looked into Audrey's warm and loving eyes. "I'm sorry," she stammered. "I don't know what came over me."

"Don't be silly," Audrey answered, "of course you do. The pain was getting so bad that you needed to release it. You couldn't do that until you felt trusting and trusted. Well you can feel that with me. I'm your friend. All right," and as she said this, she kissed Laura tenderly on the cheek. She was expecting Laura to recoil from this, but she did not. This gave Audrey some hope that their relationship might evolve into a more intimate one.

"Look," Audrey continued, sensing that Laura was not quite ready to completely let go of her apprehension, "why don't we take in a movie, unless you'd rather talk."

"No, a movie sounds good; I don't think I can talk right now," Laura answered.

"*Gone with the Wind* is playing at the Rialto."

"Sure, I haven't seen that in a movie theater before; it should be fun."

They sat in the balcony. All around them there were couples enjoying each other's company. Occasionally, Audrey would take Laura's hand in hers. Little by little, she sent signals to Laura to let her know that she was attracted to her. At first, Laura was flattered by this attention; however, it soon became obvious to her that Audrey was a lesbian. Laura's own sexuality was enough in question that she began to wonder if she was a lesbian herself. It was possible, she thought. But, it was far too intense an exploration for her to begin at the present moment.

Awakening from a Distant Dream

She realized that it was better to tell Audrey this now rather than to wait until feelings might get trampled, especially her own. Her recent experience with Danny served as a reminder to her how badly things can go wrong. After the movie, as they were leaving the theater, Laura said, "Why don't we go grab a cup of coffee and talk."

"Good idea," Audrey responded.

As they were sipping coffee in a small coffee house nearby and waiting for their deserts to arrive, Laura began, "Audrey, I think that you must know that I am not ready for any kind of intense relationship. I don't know if I can make it with another woman, and I am not ready to find out.

"Besides you're my teacher, and I want to learn from you and remain friends with you. I hope you understand. Can you still be my friend?"

Audrey looked at her silently for a long tense moment. She was quite taken aback by the maturity and acuity of mind of this young girl. She was very impressed. Tears welled up in her eyes. She grabbed both of Laura's hands in hers. "Laura, of course, I respect your feelings. I think that I am in love with you. But, yes, we can still be friends. I don't want to pressure you. Take as much time as you need. I'll leave it up to you to bring the subject up again. I'll cool it; I promise, even though it's not my style. I'm used to taking what I want. Anyhow, does that sound okay?" With that Audrey released both of Laura's hands and gently touched her face. Laura nodded and they both smiled.

Outside, Laura said, "It's time for me to go home. I had a nice time, thank you," and she took Audrey in her arms and hugged her.

"See you in class," Audrey said as Laura walked away.

Audrey looked longingly after her. She had hoped that she would be sleeping with Laura tonight. She laughed sarcastically at the folly of her own arrogance. She would

Teacher

never have suspected that she would become hooked on a student. Audrey was not happy with the prospect of being in love, for she knew only too well the heartache that definitely lay ahead.

Laura for her part was certainly attracted to Audrey, and thoroughly enjoyed her company. But, she was not ready for any kind of commitment especially one that involved her embarking on a totally new exploration of her own sexuality. She was learning to act in her own best interests. This urge to protect herself was so strong that she kept an emotional distance from her teacher. This change in attitude was so abrupt that Audrey was somewhat hurt by it, yet she retained her professional demeanor and honored Laura's feelings. In fact, she chastised herself for being so transparent and acting so foolishly.

Friendships

During her final years in high school, Laura remained relatively reclusive. Besides Audrey, she had two other friends. Friendships always proved a challenge, for her natural tendency was to seek refuge from the world that so often intimidated her by going deep within herself. She enjoyed and cherished her solitude. Being alone, however, is not always a healthy state of mind; Laura instinctively understood this.

She met Jerome in her mathematics class. Jerome was born for mathematics; it was a discipline that seemed to resonate with his nature. He was tall, lean and disjointed looking - the way most adolescent boys look. He had a kind but disturbingly self-effacing manner.

Laura sat next to Jerome in an advanced algebra class. Mathematics was a subject that Laura despised in all its forms. She was, however, required to take it in order to fulfill the graduation requirements. Laura came to depend upon him for her survival in that class. At first, her relationship with him was purely predatory but not unkindly so. However, the relationship grew to something more as they came to know and understand each other.

One day while in the middle of a particularly obtuse lesson, Laura passed Jerome a note, "I don't know what he's talking about. Help!! Laura."

Afterwards, Jerome waited for her outside the classroom. "Laura," he began, "I'd like to help you, but something came up."

"What, what's come up?" she asked.

Jerome face paled at this question. He seemed to be unsteady. Even his voice was tremulous. "I don't want to talk about it. See you later." At this he walked off and left her.

Friendships

"What was that about!" she exclaimed under her breath.

Sometime later that day, Jerome approached Laura while she was at her hall locker. "I'm sorry I was abrupt with you; I really do want to help you. Things are happening at home."

Laura knew that for Jerome this was a very difficult thing to admit. She knew that he obviously liked her and was touched by his sincerity and innocence. "It's all right," she said. "Look I have an idea. Maybe you can still help me, and you can tell me all about it. When you talk about a problem with a friend, it helps. It doesn't sound like it, but it's true. What do you say?"

Jerome looked intently at Laura. When he gazed into her eyes, he knew how he must respond. "All right," he said, "I'll meet you in study hall tomorrow."

Jerome and Laura were sitting at one of the reading tables that skirted the perimeter of the study hall. As Jerome was patiently showing Laura a sample solution to one of their math problems, Laura said, "Jerome, you look awful. You look completely pale and exhausted."

"I haven't been sleeping very well," he answered.

"Why not?"

There was a long silence. Jerome kept staring down at the papers in front of him. He was desperately trying to avoid telling Laura the truth. Finally, he spoke, "It's my parents; they're getting a divorce." His voice sounded so final; the desperation and sadness he felt were terribly apparent. Laura felt for him. She shared some of his grief.

"Is there any chance they could get back together? Parents sometimes fall out, but it doesn't mean that they can't work out their problems."

"I doubt it. I'm really not surprised; they've been fighting for years. Some of their arguments get really ugly. Their fighting sometimes make me feel quite sick," he answered.

Awakening from a Distant Dream

She grabbed his hand and held it firmly in her own. This demonstration of affection startled Jerome, who found it difficult to share his feelings with another person. Laura understood this; a realization that made her all the more compassionate. "I'm sorry," she whispered as she stroked his hair with her remaining hand. In spite of himself, Jerome surrendered to her affectionate concern. He placed his head upon her shoulder and started crying. His cries reached down into the depths of his emotions from a place where he usually avoided going. This all happened right in the middle of study hall. The other students around them looked at the pair with perplexed expressions on their faces.

From that moment on, a friendship formed between them that could not be easily broken. Laura helped Jerome explore his feelings in ways that he would be unable to do on his own, and Jerome, for his part, helped Laura see that she had an analytical side to her intellect that she had heretofore neglected.

Over time Jerome began to adjust to his parents' breakup thanks in large part to Laura's kind attention. Although he was attracted to her, or so he thought, Laura made it clear that she had no interest in that kind of relationship and enjoyed and appreciated his friendship. And so, they remained good friends. The friendship, however, remained one-sided. Although Jerome freely shared his anxieties and grief, Laura protected her inner feelings from him partly because of his gender. She still did not feel safe with men.

Sandra, on the other hand, was so unlike Laura that neither of them quite understood the nature of their attraction for each other. Sandra had placed a great deal of emphasis on her appearance and expended a prodigious amount of time in the pursuit of beauty. All of her distant, as well as immediate, goals gravitated around her looks. This behavior was sanctioned by the society at large; for, the exploitation of vanity was highly profitable.

Friendships

She envisioned a future in which she would be a world class model, or a famous Hollywood starlet, or an amazingly successful dress designer. Her monumental vanity and intense self-interest directed her behavior unerringly in that direction.

Interestingly and paradoxically, whenever they were with each other, they both seemed to be more balanced. Whenever they were in each other's company they no longer felt the need to protect themselves. They were free with each other and at their happiest.

One afternoon, while Laura and Sandra were walking home from school, Sandra seemed unusually quiet and withdrawn. "What's the matter?" Laura asked.

Sandra turned to her friend, "Do you think I'm stupid?"

"What a silly question. No, of course not, you're not stupid. Why do you ask that?"

Quite suddenly, Sandra abruptly said, "Oh Laura, I'm pregnant!"

"Pregnant, are you sure?"

"What else could it be! I haven't had a period in over five weeks, and I have the classic symptoms of morning sickness. I've done the research. How could I be so stupid? The worst is the guy's a jerk. Laura what am I going to do?"

"First, you need to come home with me. You're in no shape to go face your parents yet. Have you told them?"

"Are you kidding! They couldn't handle it. My Dad would probably throw me out of the house!"

"I hear you," Laura answered. Sandra knew about Laura's situation with her folks.

"Come on! Just come home with me for a while, all right?"

"Yeah, I think your right. Thanks Laura." Sandra threw her arms around Laura and held her close.

Awakening from a Distant Dream

As they sat in Laura's front room drinking coffee, Laura asked, "Now does the father know?"

Sandra's face grew visibly pale. She was still at the very edge of tears. Taking some deep breaths she began, "No, I haven't told him. I mean what's the point. He's not mature enough to handle it. Besides, I don't love him. What makes me angry is that we only did it once, and I didn't even enjoy it. He came so fast; I didn't have a chance. And here I am stuck with the consequences."

"Tell me about it! We're the ones that carry all the responsibility," Laura interjected. She would have liked to have gone into some detail regarding her own unsavory experiences regarding the opposite sex, but she did not want to detract from Sandra's story.

"Laura," Sandra continued, "what am I going to do?"

"Do you want the baby?"

"What the hell am I going to do with a baby! I have my whole life ahead of me. I don't want to be one of those single moms. My life would be ruined." At this point Sandra again crashed into the fuselage of her own emotions. Laura went over to her and held her in her arms for a long while. As they held each other, Laura took in the entire experience as if it was a painting. She captured the muted light of twilight as it came in through the window, the cold shadows cast by the fluorescent light in the ceiling, the books piled up chaotically on the living room table, and mostly the shape and texture of their own bodies as they were so united. Laura realized that the connection they shared was that of being women.

There seemed to be no sound except the beating of their hearts. Finally, when Sandra seemed calmer, Laura spoke, "I know everything looks awful to you right at the moment, but there are alternatives. You need to go to a clinic or seek professional help. You'll need to find out if you're really pregnant. Then you'll be able to make the right kind of decision for yourself."

Friendships

"What options do you mean, an abortion? I don't want to get an abortion. I don't think I could do it."

"I'm not suggesting anything. You need to find out what your options are. All right? I'm in no position to tell you what to do. How could I, my own life is such a mess."

"Yeah I suppose your right. Laura, would you come with me when I go?"

"Sure," Laura reassured her, "of course I will."

"Thanks, you're such a good friend."

They changed the subject, and talked about other things. Although Sandra asked Laura about her situation, Laura freely talked about her family, but, wisely, did not speak about Audrey at all. She realized that it represented a territory fraught with danger. Eventually Sandra needed to get home. Laura walked with her to the bus stop. As Sandra was boarding her bus, Laura waved to her and said, "Now don't worry, everything is going to be all right."

Sandra ultimately decided to tell her parents and went on to have the baby. Soon after, she left school and moved in with some cousins who were living in Chicago. Over time, they gradually lost touch with each other.

Laura found herself playing a very maternal and supportive role for her friends. They were decidedly unequal relationships. She knew in some part of her that this behavior did not simply stem from egalitarian notions or noble gestures of loyalty and friendship, but that it also served as a survival mechanism for herself. Inwardly, she was hurting from the pain and anxiety she suffered as a result of the separation from her parents, and her disastrous relationships with Danny and others whom she once trusted. She was understandingly protecting herself from any additional hurt so that she might have a chance to heal. She gave of herself in ways that she knew were safe. This was not a conscious strategy; it was being directed from deep within her psyche. It would not be long, however,

Awakening from a Distant Dream

before she began to come alive again to her own needs and desires.

When the time for graduation came, it was not a meaningful event to Laura.   She did not really participate in the high school social scene, and her level of maturity was such that she could not exaggerate its significance. At least, that's what she told herself.   In fact, she was terribly lonely.   She felt excluded from much of the life of her peers; she felt like a pariah. Although her isolation was, in fact, self-imposed, it did not diminish the pain it brought her. For these reasons, she could not wait until graduation was over, for her it was an unpleasant ordeal that simply reminded her of how separate she actually felt.

On the day of graduation, in the middle of June, the weather was glorious; she remained in her apartment and was miserable. In the midst of this depression, she got a call from Jerome.   It was good to hear from him. Somehow his kindness and feelings for Laura lifted up her spirits and engaged her intellect.

In spite of all the setbacks in his personal life, Jerome had decided to pursue studies in astrophysics. He had just received the notice of acceptance to the University of California at Berkeley on full scholarship. The school was impressed with his credentials.

"I want to make a living doing what I love," he told her. She wished him well. When he asked her what she planned to do, she was somewhat evasive but told him she wasn't sure. They promised to keep in touch with one another.

After they had talked, Laura wondered about her own future. Jerome's resolve triggered nascent feelings in her mind. She awakened to dormant aspirations about her own future. When she considered where her natural gifts and talents resided, she came to an obvious conclusion. "Art is what I want to do," she said to herself. It was then

Friendships

that she suddenly and impulsively decided to go to Paris and study art. When this idea came to her, it seemed to be so obviously the right choice. It released her from feeling so trapped and constrained by her present circumstances. In as much as it was her decision, it helped her feel that she was once again in control of her own destiny. It is the kind of perception that is uniquely possible within the energy and exuberance of youth, when all things seem possible and life seems to stretch infinitely forward.

Before she left, however, she thought that she should contact her parents to at least let them know what she had planned. She was surprised that they had not attempted to intervene in her life before now. They could have contacted the police and have listed her as a runaway; it was certainly within their legal rights. But they did not. In spite of this, she decided to take it upon herself to contact them before she left.

A Brief Reunion

Laura agreed to meet her Dad in front of the JC Penny's department store at the mall. She never felt comfortable in the starkly commercial environment that is a prevalent aspect of malls; she never fully understood why that was the case. She did recognize, however, that it made her feel vaguely anxious. In this general state of mind, she waited nervously for her Dad to arrive. As she stood there, she remembered all the times she used to go with her Dad shopping when she was a little girl. That was the only time they would have any opportunity to be alone together. Most of the time her mother so dominated the emotional life of the family with her incessant demands that there was little time left for simple pleasures. She could feel the overwhelming emptiness of her childhood regain a hold on her as she waited. Finally, her father arrived. She recognized his slow lumbering gate as his big-boned torso moved on its tired aching hinges.

"Dad," she greeted her father as he came up to her. They stood looking at each other from arm's length. The emotional distance that remained a formidable barrier between them had grown more or less impenetrable. Inwardly, he felt like he had made a mess out of his life. He had lived in isolation for so long that he had lost touch with even the most rudimentary form of human intimacy.

"Hello, Laura; you're looking well. I'm glad you called; I was very worried about you."

This comment hurt her deeply, for, she wondered, if that was his true feeling, why didn't he try to find her? Why did he let so much time elapse? She could have been badly injured or kidnapped or murdered. Wasn't this sufficient evidence that he didn't really care about her. These were the kinds of unnerving thoughts that played

A Brief Reunion

inside her mind. She made a valiant effort to disguise these feelings.

"Why don't we go get a cup of coffee so that we can talk?" she suggested.

Inside the crowded mall coffee shop, they sat at a small booth. Laura tried to get his attention by looking at him directly, but he kept his gaze focused away from her. This perpetuated her feeling of being abandoned by her parents. Despite this haunting perception, she had felt such pity for this man. She reminded herself that one of the reasons she decided to see him was that she was concerned about him and his welfare. This is one of the ironies of love. This is one of the grand enigmas of being human, for in response to the great sea of neglect that she faced as a child, she chose to return it with a caring heart. The bond between father and daughter is formidable and essentially inescapable.

Laura waited in vain for her father to break the eerie silence that cast such a dark shadow over them. She longed for him to tell her how he felt; she hoped that he would share his pain with her.

When that did not happen, however, something snapped within her - a powerful anger rose from her belly. Laura was no longer his little girl; she had entered the realm of the self. She no longer felt inclined to preserve cherished childhood illusions. Instead, she chose to speak the truth and restraint was thrown aside by the ferocity of her incipient rage. She could not help herself,

"Why don't you ever want to look at me!" she demanded.

Her father felt as if he had been struck dumb. His immediate response was to look all about him, dreading, above all, that other people would be watching. He raised his finger to his lips, "Shhh" he said.

"Don't try to shut me up," she answered with her bitterness dangling at the edge of every word. "Look," she continued, "I agreed to meet with you to see if we could work things out in some way, but now I see that's impossible. Why I would be so stupid to think I could talk to you now, when I could never talk to you before."

Even more formidable than the anger was the overwhelming sorrow that resided beneath it. Tears began to flood her eyes making them sparkle absurdly in the glare of the overhead fluorescent lighting. "If you care so much about me, why didn't you look for me? It's not like I'm on another planet. Don't you love me?" she implored.

He did not answer; he only stared at her dumbly. Her angry words had resurrected his immense feelings of guilt and shame. He could not answer her; he could not find the words to express the degree to which he held himself in contempt. He had become a truly miserable creature.

She wanted to be done with it once and for all. She arose abruptly from her chair and left the pathetic man at the table, for the pain she felt was unbearable. She despaired of having a relationship with either of her parents. At that moment, she vowed to never see or think about her parents again.

He wanted to call to her, to make some effort to change her mind, to win her back, but he could not. He had no frame of reference from which to act. The combined energies of his loneliness and despair had emotionally maimed him and what remained was the mere shell of a man.

That moment at the coffee shop with her father was of such import in regards to the direction her life would take that it settled into a vivid part of her subconscious reality. Often, she would find herself trying to recreate that scene in part or whole on a canvas or through her sketches. Artists are prone to introspection and are driven to represent reality within a visual framework.

It was both an act of bravery and a profound surrender to the limitations of life and human frailty. She

A Brief Reunion

was compelled to free herself - that was the nature of her burgeoning spirit. Much later in life, she would come to recognize that there was no one really to blame.

Edward sat alone for the longest time. He felt like a great dumb failure. He allowed the one person in life that he truly loved to get away. He did not blame his daughter either for her volatile behavior or her biting and hurtful words; he understood her. Secretly, within the formidable confines of his inner self, he wished her well and silently asked for her forgiveness.

Bound for Europe

She boarded the plane after checking her duffel bag at the ticket counter. She was booked on an excursion flight. All during the flight, she thought about the strange encounter she had with her father. She ran the scene over and over again through her mind. She did this until she decided to torture herself no longer.

Laura tried to think of less painful aspects of her life; her thoughts then drifted towards Jerome. She was grateful for his friendship; for, it was generous and unassuming. She examined her relationship with him and wondered what it was that she admired about him, and concluded that it was his vulnerability that she found attractive even more than his intellect. She reminded herself that she would write to him as she had promised.

Her eyes then drifted towards the window by her seat. When she looked through it, she was immediately catapulted into a state of utter astonishment. Below, the world lying beneath the clouds seemed so deceptively peaceful. "How tranquil the world looks from here," she thought to herself. Her own personal experience, however, taught her how driven humanity is by its chaotic emotions and flawed intelligence. In this way, she became caught up in her expansive thoughts and speculation. It was a relief for her to see that she could consider something larger than herself and her immediate situation. It was refreshing to remind herself that the world was a big place; she looked forward to the adventure.

Her first stop was London. From there she planned to take the boat train to Calais and ultimately travel to Paris, her final destination. She had hopes of enrolling in the prestigious Art Institute of Paris. She didn't know how this was supposed to happen, but was inexplicably certain that it would.

Bound for Europe

Laura had never been abroad. London was a good first stop for her; because, so much about it was familiar especially the language. She didn't realize how much British culture and customs had shaped America; until, she began to experience, first hand, the people of England.

When she first arrived, she found a youth hostel – a solution that fit her miniscule budget. There, she met young travelers, like herself, from all over the world. South Africans, Canadians, Australians and Germans were among the most common in this regard.

In order to better acquaint herself with London, she walked its streets. She was amazed to find that for such a cosmopolitan city, it literally closed up at 11:00 o'clock in the evening. Even the subway, which the natives call the tubes, was closed to commuters at that hour. She found this out the hard way - one evening she had to walk across a good part of the city to get back to the hostel. At first, she was terrified of the prospect of having to walk alone at night. But quite to her surprise, she was amazed to find how safe the streets were as compared to the States. Even before her journey had truly begun, she was already beginning to see the benefits of travel; for, it invited her to see the world from an entirely different perspective.

In the hostel, she lived in close quarters with other women. Directly across from her bunk, was a thin and emaciated blonde woman approaching middle-age; she had angular bony features and a discernible hardness that suggested a tough-minded personality. She was very extroverted, and not intimidated by strangers.

"Hello dear," she began as Laura was getting ready to go to bed, "my name is Sally Hobbes, what's yours?"

"Laura."

"You must be from the United States."

Laura was not used to hearing her country referred to in that way. It made it seem so distant to her. "Yeah,

Awakening from a Distant Dream

I'm from the States," she said not bothering to hide her annoyance.

"Well, you don't have to get uppity with me, dear. I'm just trying to be friendly."

"It's my first time so far from home, that's all." Attempting to switch the focus away from herself, she continued, "Where are you from?"

"Johannesburg South Africa," she said with not a little pride. "What do you think of London?" she asked.

"I like it," Laura answered. "I'm enjoying myself."

"I can't stand the place. The Brits are such snobs. They look down at you, especially if you're from South Africa. They really think they're something special - God's gift. They still haven't forgiven us for breaking away from them. We're too much our own people.

"Let me put it this way, we built our own country from scratch. Before us, the place was run by savages, by tribes that knew nothing of civilization. Just between you and me, those people are quite incapable of becoming civilized. The white race can't help it if it happens to be superior. I mean we just can't stop being who we are. I'm sure you know what I'm talking about."

Laura looked at the woman intently, then she said quite abruptly, "I'm sorry to interrupt, but I do need to get some sleep," and with that she closed the light above her bed. This action made Sally inwardly furious, but she couldn't say anything without making a complete fool of herself.

The next morning Laura quickly got dressed and left the hostel to explore the city with a tour book in her hand. Her first stop was Trafalgar Square. The sky was steeped in gray and it caste a somber shadow on everything. As she was standing near the famous monument, she was approached by a young black man with the most vivid and vibrant skin color she had ever seen. His dress was African. He had a certain vivacity that seemed to reside predominantly in his eyes.

Bound for Europe

He extended his hand and said, "Excuse me, but I couldn't help noticing you. I see that you are a tourist like me. You're not English are you?"

Laura could not help noticing that his English was impeccable. Although she would have liked to be cool and aloof, she found his warmth very contagious. "No I'm not, I'm American. How did you know that I am a tourist?"

"Oh, that's easy.   Residents are obviously comfortable in their surroundings, while we feel self-conscious. We're guests. My homeland is Nigeria. It is such a poor country that I have spent much time abroad trying to get an education. I've met many Americans but you seem different."

"How do you mean?" Laura asked. She found herself intrigued by this man.

"You're not pushy. You don't carry yourself in a way that demands attention; that demands that your needs be instantly met. Americans, seem to feel that their money entitles them. You are not that way. I don't mean to offend your people; it's just that I've always experienced them that way.

"Americans are also so oblivious of their surroundings. Worse, I think they are offended if the culture of the country they're in does not mimic their own. I bet that's the reason why there are so many McDonald's restaurants around the world - it's to make Americans feel comfortable no matter where they might be. You, on the other hand, are very observant and appreciative. Wait, that's it; I bet that you're an artist."

"Now how can you possibly know so much about me when we just met?"

"That's simple; it's all in your eyes. A person's capacity for love or hate or cruelty or indifference is all right there in their eyes. It's obvious; you just have to know how to read them. As an artist you know all that. You are an artist aren't you?"

Awakening from a Distant Dream

Laura nodded. She was very impressed and definitely awestruck by this man's ability to "read" her. At that moment she realized how right she was in deciding to travel. Her mind and heart had become hungry and desperate for exposure to human experience in new and unexpected surroundings. She needed to feel and taste not only her immediate environment but to appreciate the essence of humanity itself. "I'm Laura, what's your name?"

"Yes, of course, I'm sorry; my name is Faseil Sambutu. I hope I haven't embarrassed you. I do go on sometimes."

"No," she answered, "not at all. Faseil, what do you do?"

"I'm a student - a perpetual one at that. I'm studying to be an economist. My country is in such a mess. It needs all the experts it can get. Funny as it may sound, I don't have enough of an appreciation for money." He laughed; they both laughed. "And you?"

"I'm going to Paris to study."

"Art is such an admirable profession. Do you paint?"

"Yes, and I do some sculpture. One of my teachers turned me on to art. Without her, I would never have realized my own gifts. Did you have anyone like that for you?"

"Yes, I do; he is my uncle, my father's brother. He showed me that there is nothing wrong in deriving pleasure from life. You see my parents are devout Christians. Their ancestors were converted by white missionaries." When he said this he seemed to sneer.

"What's the matter Faseil, your whole expression changed?"

"Forgive me, but whenever I think of the white colonialists and the hypocrisy of the white man's religion, it makes my blood boil. I don't like to feel that way, but I can't help it. Anyway, my uncle was a journalist. He often took me traveling with him. He taught me so much about the world - especially that it is big and out there for me. He taught me to go after what I wanted.   It's not easy sometimes. Do you know what I mean?"

"I do, as a matter of fact I think that's what I'm learning right now.   Sometimes I feel so sure of myself and what I want.   Other times I feel so vulnerable and frightened that I feel like crawling into a cave and hiding from it all. The world can be so cruel!"

Faseil nodded, "I know that only too well. Look, I've nothing to do this afternoon; would you mind if I showed you some of this city? I've come to know it quite well."

"Sure, that would be nice," Laura answered quite surprised at her own openness. Laura never felt so at ease with another person, especially with someone she had just met.   She did not feel the usual pressure of unspoken expectations that often comes with having any kind of relationship with a male.   They walked together through many different areas of London. Faseil was knowledgeable about the city and took great pains to show Laura as much as he could. They went to Kensington Gardens, Piccadilly Circus and the Tate Museum. At the Tate, Faseil enjoyed Laura's expressions of joy and appreciation as they meandered through the many galleries.

"You seemed to be particularly interested in the impressionists. Is that true?"

"Yes, exactly, especially the way they manage to capture the emotions and paint them so vividly astonishes me – especially Van Gogh and Renoir.   They are my favorites. I so want to be able to do that."

"I believe you will."

"Really?"

"Yes, I don't know how I know this, but I'm convinced of it."

"Thank you," she answered feeling very taken by such kind words.

Awakening from a Distant Dream

When they were both getting quite exhausted Faseil asked, "Laura, where do you live?" Immediately he sensed her reluctance to tell him. He could feel her subtly withdraw emotionally from him. This reaction angered him, "You're too much!"

"What do you mean?"

"I'll wager you think that I have designs on you; that I have ulterior motives; that I have some hidden agenda. Let me put your mind at ease; I'm gay and you don't interest me a bit that way. Does that make you feel better? Can't you tell what my intentions are?"

Laura saw that his feelings were hurt, and she understood why. "I'm sorry," she said. "You're right; I was suspicious of your intentions. That's the way I was taught - to be fearful and distrustful of strangers. You don't deserve that. You have been very kind to me; I apologize. Will you forgive me?"

Faseil looked into her deep brown eyes and saw the sincerity there. He relented. "All right. But you should pay more attention, especially if you want to be an artist. You must be aware of the rich details of human expression. Can you understand that?" She nodded. "Well, I must be going. Perhaps we'll see each other again." Before she could protest, he was gone.

That evening Laura cried. Her tears were concerning her own folly. Faseil was correct. He was so perceptive; it amazed her. She felt like such a dolt in comparison. She had never met anyone quite like him. She had to shed some of that selfishness that had become a significant part of her emotional apparel. She knew that it was partly due to the side effects of her cumulative traumatic experiences. It is also a cultural impediment that Americans seem to display whenever they're abroad - the sense that whatever seems foreign is somehow dangerous regardless of what reality might teach. Beneath the tears, however, was the revelation that she had done a good thing for herself leaving her homeland, or at least it seemed so at this time.

Over the next couple of days occupied with sightseeing, Laura had grown restless and decided that it was time to journey onward to Paris. She was filled with excitement and a kind of dreamy expectation about the future. She had visions in her mind of the rich textures of Van Gogh's paintings. She was enamored of that kind of almost insatiable passion. She yearned to be able to express her own sensuality and involvement with beauty in that way. It is that yearning for perfect expression, for a direct involvement with life through the vehicle of art that drives artists to distraction. It is what makes them unsettled and so relentlessly unrealistic.

The ferry trip across the Channel was long. The water was terribly choppy and made the large ship dance as if it was a mere child's paper boat. Laura did not pay enough to get a seat. She tried to make herself as comfortable as she could on the hard wooden deck. She was not alone; there were young people all around her in the same situation.

Next to her was a young woman from Australia. They smiled at each other. The woman extended her hand, "Hi," she said in a great booming voice that counterbalanced her diminutive proportions, "my name is Elizabeth, Elizabeth Waters, what's yours?"

"Laura," she answered, purposefully excluding her last name. She didn't know exactly why she did that. One possible reason was the fact that she found the woman a bit overbearing. At least, that was her initial explanation. In fact, she was still such a neophyte when it came to travel that she felt safer revealing only her first name.

Laura, however, was gradually learning to give people more of a chance to show themselves than she was used to doing. She was beginning to realize that this could be done without sacrificing one's own security or sense of self. She was learning to trust.

"Laura, where are you off to?"

"Paris, I'm going to Paris."

"Paris, such a lovely city. I'm going to Naples. I've a boyfriend there. A luscious male stud," as she said this she licked her lips. Laura couldn't help but smile at this hyperbole. "I hope you don't think I'm being too forward?

"Men always complain to me about that. But look at me, I'm so small," pointing to her breasts, "I've got to do something to offset them, you know." At this, she threw her head back and laughed; it was a forced and boisterous cackle.

Laura thought for a moment. She made an effort not to be judgmental; she knew only too well how harmful that attitude could be. "I think it's important to be yourself."

"Why thank you dear; that is such a lovely thing to say."

Laura tried to have a conversation with Elizabeth, but it was difficult for her to get a word in, for the woman was so self-absorbed. As Elizabeth continued talking, her words seemed to melt into each other and eventually became entirely incoherent. In Laura's mind it was likened to listening to the sounds of a babbling brook; this image amused her. Soon Laura drifted off to sleep.

When she awoke the following morning, the dawn was breaking, and she went out into the open air. The sun was rising in the East and the sky was tumultuous with chaotic wind and wild with color. She was awed by the awesome beauty that permeates the natural world. It seemed like a wondrous canvas to her - filled with startling colors. "I want to be able to capture that," she said to herself, as her heart felt lightened with the power of life.

Paris

As soon as she came into Paris on the train, she knew immediately that this city would be all that she had ever hoped for. The architects of the city must have had sensuality residing in their bones; it seemed to be shaped and constructed with a woman in mind. The way the Seine danced through it, the way the light fell upon it, the way the city radiated out form its center; all these characteristics were only a partial explanation for the allure of Paris. It is a city that seemed to be exquisitely designed for human habitation.

Paris exerts an inextricable hold on the young. Laura had never before fallen in love with a place before. Her first stop was Montmartre where she looked for rooms. Along the narrow winding streets she saw the bicyclists, the women going to market; she smelled the aroma of French bread and cheese everywhere. This new world seemed so much more present and sensuous to her than anywhere she had ever been. It was as if a great door to her senses had been pried open and the world quickly rushed in. She felt alive in a wholly different way.

What she was not prepared for, however, was the arrogance of Parisians. Parisians hold on to their language like obsessed bankers protect their wealth. They are predictably insufferable when tourists fail to speak impeccable French. Although Laura bravely struggled with the language so as to learn it more completely, she was confronted everywhere by the rude impatience of shopkeepers and waiters and alleged public servants. She castigated herself for not having been better prepared.

The concierge of a group of apartments advertising a vacancy, seemed contemptuous of Laura's nationality, and seemingly took her money with reluctance. What Laura did not understand was that all this was contrived and insincere, for foreign tourists were vital to the Parisian

Awakening from a Distant Dream

economy. This was simply a self-serving game Parisians played to avoid facing the reality of their own dependence upon the largesse that tourism provides. The French are very serious about their politics, almost zealots, and their political self-esteem remains scarred from their collective behavior during World War II. Since the Americans were their liberators, it is only natural, in a perverse human way, to find fault with them.

Americans for their part usually travel within the cocoon of their own culture. They are characteristically ignorant of any language except their own, and often make no attempt to embrace the culture that they are in. They find anything not American inherently suspicious and often inferior to their own sensibilities. It is a kind of arrogance that comes with cultural isolation and unquestioned economic power. America, after having helped destroy a good part of European infrastructure during World War II, helped rebuild it and served as an unwitting model for European development. The French have still not gotten over that reality.

Laura was not that concerned about this obnoxious attitude; she came to Paris for the city itself, to luxuriate in its history, to absorb its culture and, most importantly, to perfect her art. She knew where she was to go first - Notre Dame and then the Louvre. The first day, however, she was so exhausted that she slept. It was a fitful sleep in which she dreamed of the masters, Van Gogh and Renoir. In her dream, she was their student. They constantly scolded and ridiculed her about her skill and her adeptness but mostly about her passion. "Where is your passion!" Vincent screamed, "Have you stored it in a closet and forgotten where you put it. Find the damn thing! Otherwise these lessons are quite pointless." He picked up the canvas she was working on, looked at it scornfully and begin to tear it to pieces. This left Laura in tears. It was at this point that she awakened.

Paris

One of the first things she did when she first got up was to go to the window and look out just to convince herself that it wasn't a dream and that she really was in Paris. Outside she saw a distinctly Parisian scene. On the narrow street there was the ordinary traffic and noise of cars and trucks, but along with them were many bicycles. She saw many women on bicycles carrying groceries in baskets hanging from the handlebars. She marveled at how attractive these women were. They seemed so unpretentious going about the business of life. They dressed so exquisitely, ever mindful of their gender. Laura could not tell to what extent these perceptions were due to her own awakening feelings of personal liberation.

After long moments of such revelry, she got dressed and ventured down the stairs to the outside. When she looked at herself in the mirror, she realized that her wardrobe was totally inadequate for this city and that she needed to purchase clothes, especially dresses that were more appropriate for this demanding city.

Before going to Notre Dame, she decided to simply walk the streets for a while. One of the things that thoroughly surprised her was the sheer number of bookstores in Paris. And unlike those in America, they carried many political titles that were always on display. "The French are such political animals," she thought to herself. After a number of hours of walking about, she tried her best to practice her French to get directions to Notre Dame. She could have relied exclusively on maps of the city, but she decided to throw herself into the fray. Finally, she found her way onto the Metro, the Parisian subway.

When she first looked upon Notre Dame, she was struck by its sheer magnificence. She felt a little breathless as her eyes and brain attempted to take in all the subtle and sublime details of its architecture. She became so emotional that she felt like crying. In spite of her efforts to control her feelings, tiny shimmering tears glided down her cheeks. Her eyes were bright like caldrons. She felt her heart expand inside her chest and usurp her entire body with its raucous beating. She felt breathless and light as the air around her. That cathedral became the only thing in the universe besides herself. In the midst of these powerful sensations, she remembered her dream and Van Gogh's admonition. At that moment she was touched by a kind of happiness she had never known before. She was an artist. Nothing could dissuade her now.

Inside of her, a metamorphosis had occurred. She knew suddenly where her life would take her. It was as if that vague trepidation about the future and the apparently unknown had been replaced by an indefinable feeling of certainty. She felt that she was ready to take it all on. Her love, her devotion, her sense of purpose was wedded to art. It was like she had covered herself with a kind of armor. With it on, she felt strangely secure and, more importantly, fully alive and sentient.

When Laura returned to her apartment that evening, she felt remarkably light-headed. She bought a bottle of red wine, French bread and cheese and celebrated her new-found resolve. She welcomed joy into her heart, and celebrated having taken her own life in hand. She lied there breathlessly awaiting the future and in a superbly drunken state of mind, drifted off to a sweet, sweet sleep. That night her dream was like a huge canvas adorned with painted clouds. Not stationary clouds, but clouds that drifted across her field of vision - clouds that captured the light of the day and with its derived energy constantly changed form. Those clouds masterfully displayed light, form and texture, and were a measure of her nascent purity of spirit and held out a great optimism towards the future.

The next day she visited the Louvre. She was amazed at the monumental size of the exhibits. She had

Paris

never seen so much in one place; to her, it was magnificent. She found some affinity and felt some resonance with all the various schools of painters from the classicists, the abstractionists, the renaissance masters, the cubists, etc. Her heart and her mind seemed to occupy a place together in some heightened terrain in the topography of her consciousness, but the real sense of revelation and euphoria came as soon as she entered the realm of the impressionists.

It was as if the inner souls of these masters had been extracted from them and transferred directly to canvas. She felt that they were all present with her in that room. "How filled with life," she thought. She was envious not so much of their skill, but how unafraid they were of their own deepest emotions and passions. Now she understood why Van Gogh was not successful in ordinary life. Just seeing what his eyes saw, was enough.

Laura found herself standing not only in the middle of a large room in the Louvre imbibing the impressionists, but also in the center of her own being. She, at last, was within the vortex of the fiery tempest of her own emotions. She realized that she did not have to be afraid of her own power. She was amazed at how calm it was in the center of it all.

When she was all filled up and could not absorb any more, she was on her way out of the museum when she bumped into a young art student sitting on the floor holding a sketch pad. He was copying one of Raphael's master works. "Excuse me," she said.

He was ready to be annoyed; until, he looked up and caught the radiance coming from her. He stopped breathing momentarily. This caused a strange pallor to rush across his face. He smiled foolishly. Laura could not help but smile back. "That's quite all right," he answered. His English was excellent. Laura was relieved; she did not have to struggle with French.

They both decided that they could not walk away from each other. Laura continued, "That's beautiful."

Awakening from a Distant Dream

"Oh contraire, I hate this. I'm a student. This is required," he pointed to his sketch with disdain. "You are a tourist, no?"

"Yes, I am from America, but I have come to Paris to learn."

"To learn, what?" he asked with a quizzical expression on his face.

"Oh sorry, of course; I want to be an artist."

His face brightened, "Oh forgive me," he said as he stood up and extended his hand, "I am Marcel."

"Laura," she responded.

"Where do you study?"

"The Art Institute of Paris, or so I hope; my plan is to become a student there."

"That's amazing," he said, "that's where I am a student." They looked at each other steadily. It was a moment of mutual recognition. "I'm going to the Café Printemps nearby to meet my friends. Would you like to come with me? They will all be your fellow students soon enough."

Laura felt a little overwhelmed. The whole world seemed to be opening up to her in the most unexpected ways. "What a remarkable coincidence, or is it?" she thought. Ever since she left the States, it seemed that she also left behind a very provincial state of mind and being. "All right," she said, "I'd love to."

The cafe was alive with people. The patrons seated about the tables were relaxed yet very animated with conversation. It had an intimate quality about it that Laura never experienced before. She found herself focusing her artistic eye and temperament upon her surroundings. It was if she was setting up her canvas and paints and easel and attempting to capture the moment in exquisite detail. She noted the effect of sunlight and shadows on the features of the people seated around the tables, the play of emotions on their faces, the positions and language of their bodies and the textures and shapes of the tables and chairs. She was no longer satisfied with a simple passive record of events. She found herself intimately attached to her surroundings - no longer an inept passenger in the lives of others.

Marcel looked at her and smiled. He seemed to know what she was about, or, at least, that he understood what she was feeling at the moment. "Let me introduce you to my friends." He took her hand and led her to a table that was on the sidewalk. The way he took her hand made Laura shiver. His touch was so delicate and inviting, yet it was assertive. She could not help but oblige him. The three seated at the table were involved in a lively discussion when Marcel interrupted them. "Laura this is Jean, Henri and Marie. This is Laura. Laura is from America." Laura could not help but notice the look of disdain that seemed to brush momentarily across Marie's face. "She plans to be a student with us."

The three took turns greeting Laura. She was a little surprised at the coldness of Marie's greeting, and the stiff posture her entire body seemed to assume. In contrast, both Henri and Jean were very friendly, affable and decidedly charming.

"Laura," Henri began, "so you have come to Paris to study art. That's interesting; my goal is to go to New York to study there. I guess one always desires what one does not have.

"Your timing is superb; because we were just discussing American politics. What do you think about your country's involvement in Vietnam?"

"Oh give it up, Henri," Jean interrupted, "don't be such a bore. We all know that you're just trying to draw her into a debate so that you can sound off. Why would she give a damn about your politics; she doesn't even know you! Don't mind him. He can't help himself. Would you like some wine?"

Laura quickly answered, "Sure!" She found herself looking directly and intently into the eyes of everyone including Marie. She felt a kind of intimacy she was not used to.

Marie, however, would not let the conversation regarding politics die. "I think Sartre was completely right in his demand for the setting up of a war crimes tribunal. It's no less than genocide what's happening over there. They have to be stopped." There was fire in Marie's eyes as she looked unabashedly in Laura's direction. Marie saw Laura as an enemy and, more importantly, a potential rival for Marcel's affections. "Laura, what do you think?"

Laura saw that the group was very consumed about America's involvement in Vietnam. They were all unabashedly opposed to it. Part of the severity of this feeling stemmed from guilt over France's own colonial past. She felt horribly self-conscious about her own ignorance. Inwardly, she felt this to be inexcusable. Not that she felt any desire to defend her country's politics, since there was little of that she could influence, but at least she should be more aware of the facts and be able to express herself intelligently. It reminded her of the years of her own isolation.

"I must confess that I don't understand it enough to make any intelligent comment one way or the other."

Before Marie could respond, Marcel intervened, "Marie, let's change the subject. Laura is our guest, and besides I find the whole political situation confusing myself."

When the conversation necessarily drifted to art, the center of their passions, it felt as if they were gravitating to the core of her being. About art, she was insatiable. They talked with a lustful energy about their classes, their works in progress and their own frustrations and struggle with that elusive discipline. She tried to absorb every word, every nuance. She so longed to be one of them, to be accepted as a fellow artist. The hours passed quickly. There was a fragrance in their passing. Her feelings were so intense and palpable that she could have cut into them with a knife.

Paris

Not infrequently, she looked into Marcel's eyes. There seemed to be so much room in them for her. They were so welcoming of her burgeoning desire.

The group was beginning to grow restless. Marcel rose from his chair and reached for Laura's hand, "Come," he said, "let's go." Laura responded without thinking. Marie's eyes flashed with near explosive jealousy, but it was tempered by her inexplicable attraction to Laura. She had this feeling, in spite of herself. They all liked her. She did not fit their idea of how an American was supposed to be.

It is as if the need to belong that runs so strongly in the human psyche requires enemies to strengthen the bond between kindred spirits. An enemy takes on characteristics that enable the hatred whether or not these characteristics actually exist. It is only among the few, in whom reason can prevail over these tendencies to demonize and hate, that the need for enemies becomes superfluous. It is over the ignorant and ignorance itself that demagogues hold sway. Such has been the condition of human civilizations from their beginnings.

The night was lucid and warm. The city seemed transparent and comforting. It had welcoming arms big enough to embrace all its inhabitants. Marcel walked with Laura along the Seine. The river flowed through Paris and seemed inseparable from it.

Suddenly, Marcel turned around to face her, put his arms around her and kissed her full on the lips. His kiss was prolonged and exuberant; Laura felt as if she was physically melting into his embrace. Marcel's hand glided down her body softly caressing the texture and shape of her flesh, igniting it with desire. Her genitals responded like the flower to the arrival of a bee who serves as the inadvertent carrier of its seeds.

Awakening from a Distant Dream

The wine and the sweetness of the unfolding darkness came together with the character of her feelings and conspired to shatter Laura's emotional defenses. She was ready for love. She was ready to be consumed and invigorated by its power. She was ready for the demands it would invariably make on her. She would have gladly given herself right there to him without hesitation or shame.

She had already come. It was magnificent in both its power and completeness. Marcel was behind her as she was on her side. He was in the very vortex of his maleness - ready to deposit his sperm in her. As this was going on, she found her attention drawn to one of Marcel's sketches taped haphazardly to the wall. It obviously represented a work in progress. There, suspended before her, was a representation of the essence of the artist's soul. It was a drawing of a woman sitting alone on a park bench nursing her baby. She felt the simplicity of his heart and his humanity. She could smell the fragrance of the daylight that infused the scene, and the joy of the woman with her child clinging to her.

She loved him. As this realization flashed through her mind, her body responded to him, and quite to her amazement she came again precisely when he did. She knew that Marcel certainly had experience with women. She wanted to find out more about him, but before she could even speak to him, he was fast asleep. As she lied there awake, her eyes moved around the room trying to take in as much as she could. Marcel's paintings adorned the walls. Many of these were abstract pieces. In Laura's judgment, they seemed very sensuous and brilliantly rendered; they appeared to foreshadow a brilliant career for such a gifted artist. His work seemed to have a calming effect upon her and it was not long before she fell asleep herself.

Paris

The next morning, Laura woke up in a panic. "What have I done," she thought. She remembered that she didn't use any birth control and neither did he. She turned her head to see his boyish face. She did love him, but something was wrong; it all felt ill-timed and premature.

She remembered her feelings about Danny. Then, she had an excuse for her reservations. He turned out to be an obnoxious and sadistic bastard. But now she was beside a tender and sensitive young man - an artist like herself. Yet, she felt gripped by a kind of incompleteness, for her desire was only partly satisfied. "There must be something wrong with me," she thought. Her body felt satiated, but her emotions were plagued by some inchoate source of emptiness and dread. She felt alone. What scared her was that it seemed like an incurable kind of loneliness.

The panic she felt did not subside. Rather it seemed to grow worse as she wrestled with her feelings. Quickly, she got dressed and left him. He did not stir, for he was sound asleep. She knew by the softness of his features that he had what he wanted. She envied him for his simplicity; the ease with which he found and recognized his pleasure and his place in the world.

As soon as she walked into the cool Parisian morning, however, she felt better. The rhythm of walking and the sights and sounds of others in the world helped bring balance to her emotions. She soon fell back on her own resources. "I must be more careful!" she chastised herself. After a while, she got in touch with how hungry she had become. She walked into a bakery and bought some fresh bread, croissants and butter.

In the comfort of her own apartment, she had a simple breakfast. The fresh bread felt so sensuous in her mouth. It reminded her of the love she had made the night before. Afterwards, she crawled underneath the covers of her bed and went to sleep. In her sleep, she dreamt a remarkable dream.

Awakening from a Distant Dream

She was putting on her clothes. She did not know what to wear. When she opened up her clothes closet, everything seemed to be mismatched. Try as she would, she could not find any compatible clothes. She finally relented and put on clothes randomly without regard for style or fashion.

She was walking down the street of a strange place. Everyone that walked by had human bodies but sported animal heads. She passed a candy store that she could not resist. She went in. Inside, it was a magnificent place with chocolate delights of all manner and form. They were piled high up to the ceiling. There was no one else in the store but herself and the salesman who had the head of a hyena approached her, "Can I help you?" he asked and then began to laugh.

"No thank you," she replied, "I'm just looking." She continued to browse. She finally stopped by a display where there was nothing but chocolate coated representations of human genitalia. She picked up and fondled many of them but would not take a bite out of any.

"You can have your pick my dear," the clerk bellowed.

She looked and looked but could not make up her mind, and finally ran out of the store feeling exceedingly distressed. This awakened her.

The emotion that held her in its grasp was an anxious sense of dread and foreboding that had at its source a momentous confusion - that part of the dream was clear. She suddenly felt homesick and alone and would have liked to call someone back home in the States. Her thoughts went first to Jerome, her high school friend, but finally rested on Audrey. She knew that Audrey would understand. She would probably say those words of reassurance and empathy that Laura needed to hear, but her pride would not permit it. Ultimately, exhaustion drove her back into a fitful sleep.

Paris

Laura felt somewhat uncertain about her prospect of getting into the Art Institute of Paris; since, she never queried the institute regarding available student slots or completed an application. Luck seemed to have been with her; however, for when she did go to the Institute to apply, they had an opening. To even be considered, she was required to produce a portfolio for evaluation prior to being considered for an interview. She had anticipated this before she traveled and had brought what she considered to be her best work with her. It took the admissions committee two weeks to make their decision. Although they found her work flawed, they saw this as a result of her inexperience, and they all could see an underlying passion and unique talent. It was this that convinced them to accept her on probation, if she passed her interview.

Laura sat opposite two members of the admissions committee, Francois Depuis and Georges Lemans. Georges began, "Welcome Laura. Tell us why do you want to be an artist?"

Laura was not surprised by this question. "I have always been very aware of my surroundings and acutely aware of all the effects that form and texture, light and shadow have on objects. But I did not always know that I was destined to be an artist. That came to me thanks to a wonderful art teacher I had in high school. It was then that it became clear to me that my passion for living was tied to art. I now know that I cannot live without it."

Both Georges and Francois were impressed with this answer; although, their expressions remained completely neutral.

Francois asked, "Why do you want to study art so far from your home?"

"I have always imagined Paris to be the city of art. I also have heard so much about your Institute. I must tell

Awakening from a Distant Dream

you that these feelings about Paris were confirmed when I arrived here. I can't tell you how hungry I am to learn."

Francois continued, "Tell us why you think we should accept you as a student?"

"Because," Laura began, "I'm ready to learn and will work very hard to get what I want and need. I am certain that I will succeed; art is very much a part of me. I cannot imagine myself without it."

Georges asked, "Do you have any questions for us?"

Laura thought deeply about this and finally said, "No, not really. This is the place I want to be and if you'd give me the chance, I know you won't regret it."

Georges and Francois looked at each other and Georges spoke, "Laura, thank you. We'll make a decision in a few days and will let you know."

When Laura left the interview, she felt surprised at how short it was. She took this as an optimistic sign and was confident that she would get in; although, she didn't quite understand exactly why she felt this way.

Her first days as an art student were full of promise. Her mind was a receptive vehicle in which an entire universe of thought and perception was introduced. She was beginning to learn how to look at art, interpret it and most importantly focus her own emotions, individuality and spirit into its creation.

Marcel was in a number of her classes. She, however, remained aloof. Inwardly, she was hoping that that he would try to break through her apparent coldness. She was, in fact, testing him; she wanted to see where his true affections were. He kept his distance.

Marcel could not fathom Laura's behavior. He could only presume that Laura kept her distance; because, she did not care for him. He came to this conclusion on account of his overblown and fragile ego, as one would expect for a man of his age. Such is often the way with the male psyche – it is such a vain and fragile quantity. They were both involved in an elaborate dance that was based on false premises and unfounded assumptions.

Quite surprisingly, Laura found herself becoming good friends with Henri. He had no illusions about himself. He seemed quite content with who he was. Although he seemed ordinary in appearance and intellect, his work was magnificent. Henri was a sculptor. He did much of his work in clay. Laura would often get caught up watching him work. He labored with such complete abandon and precision that the world stopped around him. She would observe in awe as the dumb spirit of the clay took on the will, vitality and force of its creator.

"Henri, your work takes my breath away," she once told Henri as they were taking a break from their studies.

"Thank you, Laura," he replied, "you are very kind. It is interesting that you say that, for most of the time I feel very frustrated. The clay seems to be so stubborn to my advances."

Laura thought that his comment was an interesting way to describe his own internal experience. As Laura looked at Henri, she noted very interesting feelings going on within her. Henri did not have Marcel's exquisite and fine features. Instead of a well-crafted aquiline nose, Henri's nose was broad and bulbous. His hair was chaotic and obviously thinning at a rapid rate. Gradually, as Laura got to know him, she realized that her own artistic mind began to reshape his outward appearance to conform to the beauty that she saw in his soul. In fact, Henri was beginning to grow quite beautiful to her. Marcel, however, began to take on outward characteristics that reminded Laura of his vanity, shallowness and in some ways stupidity. Whether or not these perceptions conformed to Marcel's real character, Laura certainly was convincing herself that they were true.

Awakening from a Distant Dream

Laura realized, as her introduction to art grew more and more intense, that her medium was painting. It was color and light that transfixed her perceptions. It was the interplay of shadow and form that engrossed her. The opportunity to create color and its effects intrigued her and dominated her quest for artistic perfection. It was that quest that produced a lonely and often merciless struggle.

The subject that dominated her early excursions in painting was Paris - the city that she adored. It was a city that brought to her heart an inexplicable joy. Often in the evenings, especially during spring and summer, she walked its streets looking for inspiration. That inspiration was never very far away.

During these excursions, she made mental notes of everything that she observed. She watched the way people dressed, the way they interacted, the way they carried themselves. She observed the subtleties of texture and lighting and color. Of course, this kind of vision came naturally to her, but her studies had helped her bring this gift to consciousness and allowed her to sharpen her abilities by disciplining them. Whenever possible, she would make quick sketches trying to encapsulate any unique and new discovery.

It was not uncommon for her to stop by a seemingly ordinary event like a child taking a drink from a public water fountain during the early evening while the light was muted by the oblique rays of the setting sun, and become transfixed by the way light impinged upon it and affected the texture and even the apparent substance of the scene. A greater and greater portion of her day became filled with these dream-like observations. Art and its perceptions were becoming more and more a part of her everyday conscious life. No activity or interaction seemed ordinary to her anymore.

Her apartment was quickly transformed into a studio. All of the other details of her life became ancillary to her art. Chaos swirled around her paints and easel and canvases. But within the zone of her creations, there existed an atmosphere of clarity and passion. Within that small and limited space, there was evidence of real work - grounded and true. Nutrition, sleep and friendship all became secondary to her focus. Her inner goal was not to represent reality, but to bring out her response to it, to draw out the truly subjective nature of reality as perceived through the fluid medium of the human mind. This was a labor not unlike one of those endured by Hercules. Laura had found a vehicle of expression for her great and consuming passion for life. When she was in the vortex of that creative dance, she felt truly free and, more importantly, remarkably alive.

As time went by, Laura saw Marcel less and less; although she was still physically attracted to him. When the pull of Eros seemed too overwhelming to ignore, she would sleep with him, but it was more a passion fueled entirely out of her own desire. Whenever she was with him in a heightened state of intimacy, however, she could not escape recognizing the depth of his vanity and shallowness. In light of these conflicting emotions, her affection for him would turn off and on often in an instant. This aspect of their relationship would drive Marcel mad with a frustration that was fueled by his own internal confusion. It was not uncommon for them to end up in screaming matches with each other. Ultimately, these feelings would result in a total break with him.

Henri, on the other hand, consistently showed himself to be a good and considerate friend. He listened to her and respected her opinions. Laura noticed the softness and suppleness in his otherwise large and cumbersome frame, but most of all, she was captivated by the lucidity of his eyes. Whenever she looked into them, she saw that they were deep and almost transparent. He was free of feelings of vanity and totally lacked self-consciousness.

Awakening from a Distant Dream

Henri, unlike Marcel, was not afraid to suffer; he was willing to take risks. On more than one occasion, he made it clear to Laura that he loved her, and that he understood that she did not feel the same passion for him. In spite of that, he treasured their friendship and endured the pain.

Henri was in the process of extending his artistic repertoire to watercolor and experimenting with abstract forms. Many an hour Laura would be with Henri in his studio while he was working. She would observe, enthralled, as Henri created still-life renderings of the most ordinary objects and instilled in them a wild and explosive vitality. His colors were always ablaze but somehow delicate and controlled. She was amazed at how quickly Henri took hold of a completely new medium and placed his stamp upon it.

On one particular occasion, while she was sketching him as he was painting, she asked, "Henri, is that the way things are with you inside?" referring to his work in progress.

Henri was a little surprised by the question. He stepped back a moment to regard his work and said, "Oh, worse, far worse. I really need to discipline it in order to create at all. That is why I must be an artist. It acts like therapy for me. It's what keeps me sane. Without it, the world would make absolutely no sense to me. I know that without my art, I could not live. Can you understand what I mean?"

"Yes, yes, Henri, of course I can. For me it is different, but I do see."

Henri was visibly shaking, "Now be quiet for a while!" he admonished her as he resumed painting.

"Sorry!" she answered as she went back to her sketching.

Vertigo

At this point in her life, Laura had not really known what true love was. She had dabbled in it and flirted with it. She had explored the edges of desire and had mistaken infatuation and normal adolescent sexual vigor and curiosity for love. These were the natural inclinations of youth. She had slept with Danny and Marcel and considered having an affair with Audrey, but these were mere foretastes of love. They suggested to her the power of her emotions and introduced her to her own passion that remained inchoate and naive. This passion was formidable and, in fact, served as the engine for her motivation and drive as a painter.

This state of being, however, was all to change swiftly and irrevocably. Laura was about to pass through that door that would open her up to the immeasurable possibilities of true human intimacy. She was soon to experience the rapture of two individual souls colliding and coalescing in the unmistakable and insatiable dance of love.

She was beginning her second year at the Institute, and had already achieved a considerable reputation as a skillful and innovative painter. Her art was for the most part representational. She was drawn to creating landscapes that were infused with a human presence. The involvement of ordinary people in natural settings played heavily in her work. She was particularly intrigued by the way people interacted with and reacted to their natural surroundings and with each other. As her work progressed, her human subjects became more intimately associated with each other. Ultimately more and more of her work depicted lovers – a choice of subject matter that reflected upon her own personal maturation. Over the summer she had traveled around much of Western Europe, especially Italy, preoccupied with her art. She remained reclusive in her travels, and did not think of much else besides her work.

In the fall, she returned to classes feeling light-headed with possibilities as a direct result of having experienced a warm and productive summer. In addition, she had become top heavy with self-assurance. In the ardor of her youth, she had begun to grow pretentious about her own abilities. She began to look upon the work of her fellow students with a critical and almost acerbic eye. This attitude was recognized by her friends as haughtiness.

"What is the matter with you?" Henri asked her as they were seated in their favorite cafe after classes.

"What do you mean?" she asked.

"You're different. You seem to look down at everyone. It's like it's only your work that matters. What has happened to you over the summer?"

"I don't really know what you're talking about," she answered defensively.

"I saw you in still-life class looking at other people's work. I saw the look in your eyes - it was scornful and mean-spirited. It hurt me to see that. Do you know what I'm talking about?"

"Oh come off it Henri," she snapped back, "don't give me all that sensitive crap! You saw some of the stuff people were doing in that class didn't you? It was garbage!"

He became extremely upset; he felt that his friendship had been violated. He was filled with feelings of both hurt and rage. They pulled at him with such intensity that he could no longer speak rationally. In deference to his affection for Laura, he got up to leave.

"Henri," she said as he was walking away, "please don't go." She realized that she had hurt him with her insensitivity, but it was too late. He was gone. She was not worried about their friendship; she knew she would make it up to him. Laura returned to her apartment, went to bed, but could not sleep. She felt badly about the way she had behaved. She understood that Henri was right, but she could not seem to help herself. Her own youthful idealism had exacted a toll on her own inner gifts of empathy and compassion. It was almost as if her own realization of her burgeoning talent had become too much for her. At least that's the way it seemed. She had a very unsettling sleep. Laura had no way of knowing that all her current ideas of herself and the world around her would soon be swept away.

She was rapidly immersed in the rhythms and work habits of school once again. Greater demands were being made on her creativity. She had been introduced to most of the classic techniques except watercolor. Laura was not looking forward to the class; the medium of watercolor intimidated her.

As she was sitting in the classroom and waiting for the teacher, she recalled that the instructor was new and only recently hired. Her attention was drawn to the door as it was beginning to open. Professor Matteo Lucese entered. He was tall and lean. His hair was noticeably thinning and it was gray. He turned to look at the class with an expression that Laura would never forget. The image of his face and its depth of intelligence seemed to burn into her brain cells a persistent and indelible memory. There was nothing exceptional about his face except his eyes. She had never seen such clarity and expressiveness. Those eyes seemed to draw Laura right into them for they also suggested an inner sadness and a composure that had as it source the raw experience of living. They said everything. They were unpretentious and remarkably kind. They spoke of a life that was somehow eclipsed by nobility and wisdom.

She was in love. This was the kind of love she would never have imagined to be possible. It was a love that instantly demanded everything of her. It was a love that required her to remove the many masks of her disposition and well-engineered pretentiousness. She felt the terror and joy of its possibilities. She felt hopelessly inadequate to the task. Laura would not have called these feelings the hallmark of love as she first experienced them. That would have been too much for her to bear.

For the sixty minutes of his introductory lecture, Laura heard nothing; although, she was hopelessly transfixed by the intensity of his language. She noted traces of myriad emotions as they moved across his features and subtly changed them. She was attentive to every glance, every nuance of expression as he addressed the class. Everything outside of the boundary made by the two of them became shadowy and unreal. She forgot about Henri's displeasure with her, Marcel's vanity and even her own insufferable pride in her work. It all suddenly seemed totally inconsequential.

Although the lecture passed right through her, she did notice, however, that occasionally his eyes would fall upon her and linger there for a brief and subtle moment. It made her heart weak. She felt so pliable that she was ashamed of herself. She thought it might be wise to get out of that class, but she could not. Her fate had become irretrievably altered by the power of her feelings towards this apparent stranger.

During one of her first classes with him, Laura was struggling with her paper trying to create a still-life from various kitchen items assembled on a table in the front of the room. She was so distracted that she constantly found herself looking up at him. She could not seem to help this impulse. He made his rounds of the classroom and approached her from behind. He looked carefully at what she was doing. After some time, he finally spoke.

"Laura," he said, "you are trying much too hard. I make it my business to look at my students' finished works. I have examined your portfolio and have been touched by the sensitivity and passion of your paintings. You have a definite way with paint. But, you need to be well-rounded and not imprisoned by any one medium. Here, your passion seems to have been bottled up. You need to uncork the bottle and let it out. Don't struggle with it so much. Let the medium express you." He looked at her intently. "Does what I am saying make any sense to you?"

"Yes, professor," she stammered and was barely audible.

He looked at her for a moment, smiled and walked on.

"He doesn't know why it's bottled up," she thought to herself. She struggled through the rest of the day. That evening, in the privacy of her own room, she let her recollections of him return to her. She recalled the clarity of his eyes and the quality of his speech. She felt the radiant effects of his understanding and compassion. She could not think of anything else. She turned the words he spoke over and over in her mind trying to extract some hidden meaning. She was completely lost.

Weeks went by. Every day seemed to melt into each other. Her feelings grew more intense rather than less as she had hoped. She was beginning to feel panic inundate her. She did not know what to do with these gigantic and terrifying feelings. She tried to convince herself that he was too old - that she was simply infatuated with the man and that her feelings were transient and would pass. She wished there was someone she could talk to about this, but there was no one she trusted enough to do so. She felt far too vulnerable.

Within the chaos of her own emotions, she was unable to realize that he too had fallen in love. Matteo lived alone in a small apartment. His wife had passed away some five years ago. She died of a long, debilitating and ruinous battle with breast cancer. They had no children; he

Awakening from a Distant Dream

was truly alone and was beginning to become inured to the solitary life. He had been in mourning all that time. Suddenly, however, during that brief and captivating moment when his eyes met those of Laura, he had been dragged precipitously into the present. He had no rational explanation for the instantaneous and precipitous change in his state of being upon seeing Laura for the first time. What he did realize, however, was a sense of awakening as if he had been in the midst of a deep slumber reminiscent of those feelings he had when he first met Carmella many years before. It was this realization that he found so unsettling. He, too, was terrified of his feelings, but for different reasons. The portal that love opened to him shown with brilliance, but passing through it was fraught with danger. He did not know if he were capable of sustaining another loss or the joy that love might bring for that matter.

One morning, while shaving, he looked upwards, "Carmella," he said, "I don't want to be unfaithful to you!" The image of the sweet and endearing face of his wife was beginning to grow indistinct. Time had nearly cured him of his once inconsolable grief. This made him feel very anxious and terribly guilty. "Carmella, what should I do? I am an old man. What could she possibly see in me? This is ridiculous." Being purely a matter of the heart, the voice of reason had little influence. He had fallen in love with Laura - there was no doubt. He came to the inescapable conclusion that he must act on his feelings regardless of the consequences and the uncertainty that relationship would surely bring. Since he had always lived by the dictates of his heart, he had little choice. "I'll need to speak to her," he said to himself. "I hope she doesn't take offense dealing with such a crazy old man."

Vertigo

"Laura," Matteo spoke softly as he stood behind her while she was painting with his hand briefly touching the curve of her shoulder, "I would like to see you after class."

Laura stood nervously by his desk as the other students were leaving. He pointed to a chair and said, "Please sit down." She could tell by his expression that he was nervous and had something important to tell her. This surprised her; because, she had never seen him look quite so vulnerable. At first, she thought he was going to tell her that her work was hopelessly inadequate, and that she'd probably be better served in a different profession. She waited anxiously for the bad news.

"Laura, you must forgive an old man for his foolishness. I don't know how else to say this, but to say it directly. I find you very attractive. I was wondering if you would not mind dining with me some evening. Please, you don't need to answer right away. If you're not interested, just tell me; don't spare my feelings for I have enough experience with disappointment and can accept rejection." As he said this, he pointed to his gray hair, and smiled broadly. "I know that I'm an old man, and probably should be ashamed of myself, but I do like you."

Laura stood there for a moment, immobilized. She felt as if her entire body had turned to stone and became instantly incapable of movement. Her mind, however, was rebelling with happiness. "Be discreet," she importuned herself without success. "Yes, professor, yes," she answered, "I would be more than happy to go out with you."

He looked at her with such unabashed intensity and astonishment that she felt that she would melt, then he placed his hand tenderly on her cheek. "All right then," he said, "you must come to my place tomorrow and I will cook for you. For Italians, that is the best way to begin to become acquainted, Si?"

"Si," she answered.

Awakening from a Distant Dream

Laura and Matteo acted like adolescents in preparing for the evening they would spend together. They struggled with their appearance; they were hopelessly uncertain about the clothes they would wear, and were exceedingly nervous and unsure about how they would behave or how the evening would unfold. She chose a light and airy blue summer dress that was bright but not pretentious and flattering to her body. He decided to wear tan slacks and a white short-sleeved shirt in keeping with his more conservative nature.

As she sat at the small round dining room table, she felt remarkably comfortable in his apartment. She had expected to see examples of his work adorning the apartment. Instead, she was struck by the austere surroundings reflecting a simplicity of spirit. She did note, however, that everything in his apartment was representative of a stylish taste and artistic temperament.

While she sat there with a glass of wine in hand, Matteo was busy in the kitchen preparing dinner. Her eyes became fixated on him as he was occupied with his preparations. She was absorbed by the grace and refinement of his movements. She was mesmerized by a quality of his being that she was, at first, unable to identify. She was later to realize that the aspect that she was so drawn to was his serenity and sense of quiet self-assurance. What she was falling in love with, in part, was his maturity. Like so many young people, she had regarded aging as a reality of living not worthy of consideration. She had never before witnessed firsthand the value and benefits of the cumulative impact of life experience and self-examination. Matteo was definitely a student of life.

"What are you making?" she asked.

"I'm sure that it will be of no great surprise that I'm making a pasta dish. Do you like Italian food?"

"I adore Italian food," she answered.

Vertigo

"Good," he said, "I'm glad. I just hope that you'll be forgiving of my cooking."

"I'm sure it will be wonderful," she replied.

"I think you should reserve judgment in this regard," he said with a smile.

As they sat down to eat, Matteo refilled her glass and said, "Tell me a little about yourself Laura. How did you come to be here in Paris?"

"Well, professor," "Please," he interrupted, "call me Matteo." "All right, Matteo, I came to here to study art; that is my main reason. I felt that Paris was the place to be. I grew up in Quincy, Illinois in the United States. It's not far from Chicago. Do you know anything about the States?"

"Yes, a little - I've been to New York and have some relatives in San Francisco. Once I remember stopping over in Chicago. I was struck by the architecture. But, please continue."

"Well, it's a typical suburban town."

"What makes it typical?" he asked.

"Oh everyone knows everyone or they think they do. People are very inquisitive and they love to gossip. It got so bad there that I felt like I couldn't breathe sometimes. Do you know what I mean?"

"Sure I do. It doesn't sound much different than my hometown."

"Where is that?"

"Ottaviano, near Naples. So, you came to Paris primarily for the art or to escape your upbringing?" His look betrayed an undercurrent of uncertainty; it felt to her like he was probing.

"My life is my art. I had a marvelous teacher who helped me to see how important art really is to me. And Paris, its effect on me goes without saying. I knew as soon as I arrived that it was the place where I belonged."

Awakening from a Distant Dream

Internally, Matteo marveled at the innocence and idealism of youth and how wonderfully free of the compromises and disappointments that are sure to come. "I'm relieved to hear you say that. Truthfully, from what I have seen you have much talent. It needs development, to be sure. But it is, of course, my job to help you with that. No?"

"Of course," Laura replied. Her fear of having said something terribly out of place quickly subsided, for she felt totally immersed and comforted by the warmth of his personality and demeanor.

Matteo smiled broadly. He knew himself well enough to realize that the underlying reason for his questions was an attempt to defuse his interest in her, but this was a strategy that was bound to fail. He was far too attracted, too involved, to allow reason to have the last word. This ambivalence reflected itself in his manner; inwardly, he was just as confused as ever.

Laura took advantage of the brief silence to ask, "Now tell me about yourself, Matteo?" As she said his name, she enjoyed the sensuous way it felt when pronounced and how beautiful it was to hear.

"Ever since I was a young boy, I knew what I wanted to do with my life. My family had been fishermen for generations. I used to go down to the coast and took pleasure at just observing everything around me. I was captivated by the way the light danced across the water and the clouds would always be changing and transforming the landscape. I remember vividly my excitement when I first realized that the sparkling light on the water was the result of uncountable numbers of individual reflections of the sun. I longed even then to be able to capture and recreate that experience. I guess you have to be greedy to be an artist.

"My father soon realized that my dreams and aspirations had little to do with fishing. But, thankfully, I was not the oldest son. The oldest, my brother Attilio, had the biggest burden. The first born son always took on the greatest responsibilities in that era and had a duty to fulfill his father's wishes. I was spared that responsibility."

"Do you have sisters?" Laura asked.

"I have two sisters, Angelina and Louisa; they are both younger than I. Angelina was always my favorite. I used to spend most of my time with her. Things have changed in Italy for women especially in the cities. They began to change during the war, but in the small towns and villages, I'm afraid it is much like it has always been. Women had their roles clearly defined. It was the men who were allowed to pursue their dreams." As soon as he mentioned war, he noticed that Laura appeared puzzled. "I was talking about the Second World War. I'm sorry; I sometimes forget how long ago that was. I'm showing my age.

"Anyway, I went on to become an art student, and studied in Rome as a young man. I have only recently moved to Paris. Not a very interesting life, but I have enjoyed it. I feel lucky to be next to what I love and to be doing that which inspires me. Many are not that fortunate.

"And here I am talking about myself to such a beautiful and charming young woman, who, I am sure, could find some more interesting things to do with her time." Laura realized that he said this out of perfect sincerity.

"No, no," she protested. "I am enjoying this. There are very few people who I have met that have been so true to themselves." For some reason, possibly the fact that Matteo represented the kind of father she wished she had, Laura felt remarkably open with him. Possibly because Matteo inspired a kind of trust that was completely new to her, Laura freely said, "Matteo, I like you very much. You needn't be apologetic. I'm here because I enjoy your company. I want us to know each other better and better." As she said this, a slight blush momentarily washed across her face. This did not escape the trained eyes of an artist.

Awakening from a Distant Dream

Matteo looked at her with great compassion and considerable affection. "Laura, I feel the same. It is rare that I have an opportunity to speak with someone from the heart. Artists are usually such self-indulgent and self-possessed creatures. If you would allow me to, I would like to say that I am very proud of you."

With that last comment, Laura's heart opened itself up even further like a desert bloom caressed by its first drops of spring rain. The evening went by with that singular aura of intimacy that binds lovers to each other.

At the end of the evening, Matteo walked her home. They had little to say to each other; they appreciated the silence savoring the night air. When they arrived at her front door, they looked into each other's eyes for the longest time. Impulsively, Matteo put his hands delicately around Laura's face and said, "I've enjoyed this evening so very much. Thank you." He then kissed her gently on the lips. That night, they both slept restlessly, both awakened and frightened by the prospects for the future.

Yet Another Turning Point

For weeks, Laura would linger after her classes with Matteo were over. When they were alone, he would come up to her and they would talk. Often they would go to one of the local cafes and spend long hours together. Love was tightening its powerful hold on them. They both recognized the inevitability about what they were doing, yet neither was prepared to admit what was to everyone else quite obvious. On weekends they were inseparable.

He made it his goal to show Paris to her - all aspects of the city not simply the part associated with culture and heightened emotions. "Tonight," he said, "I'm going to take you to the Pigalle. Do you know what that is?"

"Isn't that where the meat markets are?" she asked.

"Yes, meat markets, yes you could say that."

"Why are you smiling, what is so amusing about that?"

"Well, my dear, you will soon find out!"

As they walked through the district, Laura quickly realized why Matteo was so bemused by her innocent question, for the street was filled with prostitutes lined up, waiting for their clientele. This realization made her blush with embarrassment.

"I hope you don't mind," he said, "I wanted to show you all the aspects of the city. Paris is, after all, a city filled with humans of all kinds - reflecting their flaws as well as their virtues. As an artist, you should be able to represent this as well. It is beautiful in its own right."

Laura looked at him feeling a little confused. She immediately turned her attention to the scene. Her acuity of vision eagerly embraced the richness of her surroundings: the stalls with huge sides of beef and pork hanging indecorously under bright incandescent lighting and the butchers with their blood-stained aprons as testimonial to the slaughter. All this was strangely juxtaposed with the queue of prostitutes soliciting these men, weary of their trade, with their ample bodies proudly displayed. The males were torn between their work and the women who held out some promise of comfort and pleasure.

She strived towards a purity of vision and tried not to distort the reality in front of her with hasty and ill-conceived judgments. The more she used her senses in that way, the more she understood what Matteo was trying to tell her. With these thoughts in mind, she was able to visualize how she would capture this exquisite slice of humanity on canvas. Again, she was awed by this man and what he was able to show her without even the hint of pretense.

She suddenly turned to him, held his face in her hands and kissed him passionately on the lips. "I love you," she said. Matteo was both hoping for and dreading this moment. Laura surprised herself with her own behavior, for she acted purely on impulse and from the heart. He kissed her back with equal passion and a strong feeling of possessiveness. They had passed that profound boundary that separates friends and lovers. There was no going back for either of them. They looked deeply into each other's eyes and fell into that wondrous abyss that is the providence of lovers.

Matteo finally said, "What are we going to do?"

To this Laura responded, "Take me home with you."

That night the inevitable finally happened. Their first attempt at lovemaking was awkward. She was tentative and shy while he was simply "out of practice." He was not without guilt in making love to a woman so much younger than himself. Although the complexity of their feelings inhibited the intensity of their mutual pleasure, the joy of their shared intimacy was unabated – joy is paradoxical in nature and can exert its presence within a variety of settings. It was the undeniable strength of this primal feeling that convinced Laura that what she was doing was right.

Matteo, on the other hand, was intimidated by the rightness of his feelings. He had grown so used to living alone and depending solely upon his own resources that he was frightened by the prospects of all that suddenly changing. He could not help but think of his departed wife and with that came a rather unwelcomed feeling of guilt. It was a reaction that thankfully was not completely out of his control. As a mature and responsible male, he also could not help but thinking that a relationship with Laura could be an impediment to her own development.

With these thoughts in his mind, he turned towards her and said, "Laura, I don't know if we're doing the right thing?"

"What do you mean?" she asked. This statement confused her, for it seemed so much in contrast to the look of love he had in his eyes.

"You are so young. You have so much of your life in front of you. What do you want with an old man like me?"

"Don't be silly, Matteo. You know the reason as well as I; I love you. I trust you like I have never trusted anyone before. I want to be with you. You worry me when you talk like this. Don't you feel the same way about me?"

"Of course I do. You make me want to celebrate living in a way I have not felt in years."

"Then let's not worry, all right?" she insisted.

He looked at her and was immediately engulfed in the love that was evident in her eyes. He pulled her towards him and mounted her with as much tenderness as his aroused passions would allow. This time, their bodies flowed with each other along the same ineluctable current. When the rhythm of his motions was reaching its sublime conclusion, she was right there with him, and they came all over each other with such an outpouring that they were both convinced that they would surely be consumed by the intensity of their shared desire.

Afterwards, their bodies seemed to melt into each other. They were both so satiated that they were quite incapable of speech. It was only a matter of moments before they fell into a deep sleep in each other's arms.

Matteo and Laura were inextricably bound to each other. They were so lost in their shared emotions that they did not notice or pay attention to the stories that were circulating about them through the school. In spite of the gossip, however, no one interfered with them in any way, or judged their behavior as inappropriate. Laura was quite amazed about how tolerant the French were when it came to matters of the heart, for in America such overt behavior between a mature teacher and his young student would have led to very ugly consequences spawned by self-righteous attitudes. "No wonder the French see us all as prudes," she thought. Of course, like all relationships of the heart, the journey they were on was not without risks. The joy of intimacy invariably brings with it a fear of disappointment and dissolution. Nonetheless, they had both made the decision to trust each other with their hearts.

One night after intense lovemaking, Laura noticed that Matteo's face seemed taut; she felt the presence of the shadow of anxiety across his countenance. "What is the matter, Matteo?" she asked.

"Oh, it's nothing, nothing!"

"Nothing, don't tell me nothing!" she said somewhat playfully yet determined to get an answer. "What is the matter? I can see by your face that something is wrong. Now what is it? I won't leave you alone until you tell me."

Matteo could see that he would have to talk to her. He took a deep breath to bring as much air into his lungs as possible.

Yet Another Turning Point

"All right," he finally said, "I was worried about babies!"

"Babies," she said, "what about babies?"

"I have been assuming you are using protection. But, maybe that was a foolish assumption."

"What do you mean a foolish assumption? What do you take me for!   You think I'm some kind of scatter-brained American, don't you? You're worried! What about me? I'd be the one to become pregnant, not you!"

The more she turned his words over in her head, the angrier she became. She felt as if she had been betrayed. "Don't you trust me," she finally said. "I have given myself to you, and you don't even trust me! Do you think I'm trying to put something over on you?"

"No, no," he answered, "certainly not. I don't want you to become pregnant - more for your sake than mine. At my age I would make a terrible father, probably worse than no father at all. Not only because of my age, but because I have no children and no experience with being a father. I could never forgive myself if your career was cut short by a baby. Laura, you have such promise. You have the makings of a great artist. You have everything: the skill, the talent, but most of all the heart and soul of an artist. I see greatness in store for you."

Laura went into temporary shock. "You mean it?" she asked. "You mean it? You're not just saying this, are you?" completely forgetting the anger she had felt only moments ago.

"No, of course not," he answered. "You have the gift.   It should not be denied its expression or be squandered. I have watched you with great interest. I would never forgive myself if I were responsible for your failure to achieve that which is rightfully yours. Do you understand!" As he said this, he held her face tenderly in his hands and kissed her on the lips delicately, yet not without passion.

"Oh thank you!" she responded, "thank you. You don't know how important those words are to me. But, I do love you, and would be proud to have your baby!"

"Laura, there will be plenty of time for that. For now, you must promise me that you will never let your talent diminish or wither. Do you promise?"

Laura looked into his eyes, and realized that it was futile to protest. Of course, she knew in her head that he was right, but in her heart, well that was yet another matter. "Yes, yes, I promise."

"Good," he said, "that is good."

Being thrust into a thoughtful mode, Laura asked, "Matteo, you never talk about your wife. Do you miss her?"

"Yes, sometimes I miss her terribly. But I have to tell you that lately I am beginning to forget what she looked like. I feel ashamed about this, especially being an artist. I used to have such a vivid recollection of her beautiful face. I used to talk to her, but now that doesn't happen. I suppose I don't have the need any more. I hope that speaking like this doesn't make you feel uncomfortable."

"No darling, not at all. I feel flattered that you are willing to share these things with me. Obviously, you loved her very much."

"Very much," Matteo simply answered.

"Would you mind me asking you why you never had children?"

"Of course not, I have no secrets to keep from you. When we were first married, we tried very hard to have children. Unfortunately, none came. We never were able to find out why - whether the problem was mine or hers. Maybe that's a good thing. I don't know what kind of father I would have been."

"I think you would have been a wonderful father. In many ways that is what you are to me." As soon as Laura said this, she realized it may not have been a good idea to tell him that. A shadow passed over his face.

Yet Another Turning Point

"Please don't misunderstand me," Laura insisted. "It is you the man that I fell in love with, but I marvel at how many facets there are to our relationship. I hope I haven't hurt your feelings."

"I have to say that, at first, I was hurt by what you said. But that was just my own vanity that got the best of me. Honestly, I can't help but behave in a fatherly way towards you. It would be silly for me to deny this. Please, don't worry, I'm not hurt. As a matter of fact, I could say that I am flattered."

"You should be," she answered and put her arms around Matteo and kissed him. They fell into each other's sweet embrace and began communicating with their bodies instead of their intellects and entered an entirely new realm.

To a Mother, Farewell

Over the time they were together, Laura's life seemed to be filled with love and good fortune. Her joy was reflected in her art. The colors she used on her canvases had a luster and brightness that she had never used before. Her art grew more and more abstract and less representational; she was taking the kind of risks that she had never taken before . Her work was literally infused with her own passion. She never would have imagined that life could feel as good as it did.

Together with this exquisite set of emotions, Laura had that foolish inner sense of invulnerability that is so consistent with her youth. It was under such a spell of rightness and perfection that Laura decided to make it her business to become pregnant despite Matteo's profound misgivings. For this reason, she sometimes purposefully avoided taking her daily dose of birth control pills, fully realizing that this behavior would negate any protection they might have provided her.

She understood that this calculating behavior would surely provoke his anger if he should find out, for it was a definite betrayal of trust. For this reason, she decided never to tell him. Such was the state of things when she received a telegram from her father. She was alone in her apartment when she received it. She realized that it was important, and anticipated bad news. The telegram read:

"Laura, dearest. Please come home immediately; your mother is terribly ill and close to death. Dad."

Her gaze seemed to remain fixated on those words. The feeling of dread that rose up in her was nearly overwhelming. Immediately, her extremely image-oriented mind began to paint a picture of her mother lying on her death bed. The picture that she created of her mother's face was not far removed from the death-like mask she wore when she was well. She pictured the bed with its comforter neatly arranged around the woman's frail emaciated corpse. She saw vividly the tasteless picture of a black velvet clown on the wall right above the headboard, and the lamp by the bed table with the lampshade still covered with plastic. And finally, she visualized the glow of the television's phosphorescent screen flickering across her mother's passive features. These images vividly displayed in her mind's eye made her shudder, for she understood their reality only too well. But more than all of these, she recognized the fear in her father's eyes. She knew that death was also waiting for him. All these dark thoughts made her feel pale and weak. She needed the steady hand of Matteo at this moment. She called him on the telephone.

"Matteo," she said, "I need to see you right away."

"What's wrong?" he asked. "You sound terrible."

"I can't tell you over the phone. Can you come over?"

"Certainly," he said, "I'm on my way."

When he arrived at Laura's place, he saw that she was very distressed. He went to her and kissed her sweetly on the cheek, "What's the matter?"

"I got this telegram from my father. My mother is dying."

"Then you must go home to be by her side."

"But, I don't want to go."

"Don't want to go. What do you mean? It's your mother you're speaking of. Why don't you want to be with her? I don't understand you."

At first Laura could not answer his questions. It hurt her to think about her own feelings; they seemed so shallow and uncaring. Then finally, she answered, "I, I don't love her. She never has shown me any affection. I don't know her; she is a complete stranger to me. Can you understand that?"

"No Laura, honestly, I really can't. Regardless of the feelings you may or may not have for her is no excuse for not being with her. You should go. If you don't, you will come to regret it. One begins to appreciate these things only later in life. Youth is too impatient a mistress. You shouldn't let selfishness determine what action you should take."

At first, his words seemed so uncaring; she wanted to protest. But, she understood that, in truth, she felt so confused and frightened. Laura was never very good at hiding or disguising her feelings. She threw her arms around Matteo and simply started to sob. It felt as if her entire insides were coming apart. She felt as if she was about to self-destruct. "I don't know; I'm frightened. I hated the woman almost all my life, but now I feel that maybe the problem might be with me. I feel like I have betrayed her. Maybe it's all my fault. I don't know if I can face her."

"That is precisely why you must," he answered making sure that his tone was reassuring. "Neither of you are to blame; life can be messy. Look, she is your mother and that you can never change." He held on to her very tightly. "Don't punish yourself. I love you Laura. You are such a fine person; it hurts me to see you treating yourself so badly." He rocked her gently back and forth in his arms. He seemed to know instinctively what to do to help Laura through her crisis. It was moments like these that reaffirmed and strengthened the bond that existed between them.

Once she had finally calmed down enough, she looked up at him and said, "Matteo, you're right; I have to go, but I'll miss you. What am I going to do without you?"

"You'll be fine, my dear. I'll be with you even if only in spirit. Just remember to stay true to yourself. Now you must hurry for there is little time to lose. Keep in mind that I am here for you." She was tempted to ask him to come with her, but quickly concluded that it wouldn't be a good idea.

To a Mother, Farewell

She reserved a flight to the States for the next day, called her Dad and settled some other last minute business. That night they made love with such intimacy that her egg leapt out and succumbed to one of Matteo's seeds as they flooded inside of her.

Once she boarded the plane, it was if all the feelings and associations that she thought she had left behind reemerged within her consciousness. The wave of emotions she experienced were paradoxical, for in one regard she felt the singular freedom of being another anonymous person in a sea of strangers, yet she felt a desperate coldness descend upon her - a feeling profoundly understood by the truly lonely.

She did not know how she would behave upon seeing her mother. When she last saw her, she seemed to be a member of the living dead. She tried to remember happier times during her childhood. There were such occasions, but they were few and growing indistinct within the tumultuous sea of her recollections.

When she was very young, the family went on long summer excursions to New England and the South. Her mother, as a young woman, loved to swim and helped Laura learn. She remembered the long summer days on the beach. She thought she could recall her parents kissing and being playful and affectionate with each other. She tried to focus on these shadowy images as a way to help her through this very rough time. Laura was so distracted by these thoughts that she was startled when the pilot announced that they making their descent to O'Hare airport.

As she disembarked, she looked hesitatingly at the crowd of people all looking for someone they knew. Suddenly, there among the awaiting crowd, she recognized her Dad. He was different. At first, she could not place just why he seemed so different. Then, it became apparent;

he had lost a great deal of weight. His face was tired and gaunt and he looked utterly beaten by life. When their eyes met, however, a change came over him. He seemed lighter. He no longer felt so desperately alone.

"Laura!" he called out.

She walked swiftly over to his side. "Daddy," she said, as she embraced him, "I'm so sorry!"

They held on to each other momentarily. "Come," he said, "let's go get your bags. How was your flight?"

"It was all right," she replied. "You've lost weight, haven't you?"

"Yes, lots of weight, in fact. I can't say that I feel better though." Suddenly, his demeanor seemed to revert to his usual self. She could sense his retreat into himself like a frightened turtle. It's as if he could not bear to be outside himself for too long. She sensed his pain, and felt a burning compassion for the man.

While they were driving back to what used to be her home, Laura was looking intently out the window catching glimpses of her past. While many of the familiar places were gone – replaced by ever-expanding housing developments – some aspects of the neighborhood seemed immutable. She was especially impressed to see that her old school looked very much like it always did. Her musing was abruptly broken by her father's somber voice.

"Laura, the doctors say your mother hasn't long to live."

Even though she expected what he just told her, waves of shock reverberated through her body. "What does she have?" Laura asked, already knowing the answer.

"Lung cancer, she's got lung cancer. You know that cough she had. Well, it got to the point she was actually spitting up blood. She let that go on without telling me. One day I happened to see a bit of tissue she forgot to throw away. When I finally got it out of her, I insisted she go to the doctor. By the time they examined her it had already spread to other parts of her body. If only I had paid more attention!" His hands began to tighten around the wheel until his fingers became pale from the lack of circulation. His whole body quivered.

Laura had never seen her father in such a state of mind; although, she long suspected that he kept his emotions harnessed and caged like some wild untamed creature deep within himself. She touched his hand and said, "Daddy, don't blame yourself. You know it was the smoking. We both tried to convince her to quit. We'll do what we can, all right?"

"Yeah, you're right. I'm so glad you're here. Laura, I've missed you. It's funny I can tell you that now. Life is a puzzle, isn't it? For so long I've worried about you and wanted so much to tell you how much I love you and am proud of you. The time never seemed right. Your mother has dominated my life and preoccupied my thoughts for so long; it's like a large part of me went to sleep. Now, strangely, I feel freer." It was so interesting to hear her father talk like this. She almost felt embarrassed. She never imagined that he would ever reveal the depths of his inner life to her. Hearing him express his feelings of longing and frustration made her feel ignorant, terribly ignorant. She also felt ashamed, for she remembered when they last met and how insensitive she had been. She admired and appreciated the fact that he had obviously forgiven her.

As they pulled up the driveway, they both fell terribly silent. It was partly out of respect for the suffering that they would soon encounter. Laura tried to prepare herself for what she was about to see. Her mother had occupied a space in her mind that was among the darker recesses of her thinking. She tried to adopt a brave and optimistic exterior as a way to protect herself from the stark and depressing reality that she knew would soon confront her.

Awakening from a Distant Dream

In spite of her best efforts, when they passed through that front door, Laura felt her entire being enter a state of dread and panic. The layers of despair and imminent doom that embraced and filled the space around her mother seemed to swallow her whole. She fought for air. She hurried to a place of safety in her inner mind. It was that part of her being that Matteo had helped introduce her to and where his presence resided. "Matteo, Matteo," she said over and over to herself much like a mantra.

Inside the bedroom, her mother was lying fully wrapped in layers of sheets and a heavy comforter that made her appear mummy-like. Suspended from a rack next to her bed was an IV bag with a red liquid flowing from it down a long slender transparent plastic tube ending in a vein in her right arm. Her face was partially covered by a respirator. The staccato rhythm of the respirator's pump added to a strange atmosphere of unreality. She was not asleep, nor did she seem totally awake. A nurse was sitting by her bedside engrossed in the latest issue of Cosmopolitan magazine. When she heard Laura and her father walk in the room she put the magazine away, stood up, acknowledged their presence and left the room so that they could have some privacy.

Laura stepped forward timidly and moved hesitatingly towards the bed. Her mother immediately sensed her presence and her eyes tried to focus, but with difficulty. The shadow of a smile brushed across her face. Laura would never forget that momentary expression, for it captured all the longing and the loss that so exemplified their relationship to one another.

Her mother feebly held out her hand. When Laura touched it, the coldness of it seemed to run through her whole body. She felt the stark and foreboding reality of the scene usurp her equanimity - the finality of the tomb, the immensity of time, of space, of infinity all seemed to occupy the moment. That same coldness was now demanding release from her mother's weary flesh. Laura had always felt that the shadow of death was embodied in the spirit of her mother. But now she wondered how much of that sensation came from her own perceptions, for, paradoxically, the feel of her mother's touch also spoke of love and tenderness. On the edge of her own mortality and at the precipice of consciousness, the dying woman acknowledged her child and extended her last bits of energy towards her.

Laura sat down at the edge of the bed and lowered her head down. She kissed her mother tenderly on the cheek, "Mama," she said, "I love you."

Her mother stirred and her vacant eyes seemed to momentarily lose their opaqueness. Her feeble hand held onto her more tightly.

Laura felt a great surge of long-buried love inundate her senses. This feeling was tainted by the inescapable specter of pain. That pain had its origins in feelings of regret for not having seen any hint of her mother's love when she was more fully alive. She spent much of her young life despising her mother for her apparent indifference and shunned her. She carried with her that kind of inner desperation and unsatisfied longing that is a direct outcome of being denied the love and nurture of the mother at a young age.

Laura gazed at the vision of her mother on her bed barely clinging to the remains of her life with all the medical gadgetry sustaining her. She watched her intently as she periodically struggled for air. During those episodes, Ruth would make vain attempts to pull the mask off of her face. Laura looked at life's end and her artist eyes attempted to capture its poignancy and drama. Death is, after all, a rapacious beast that spares not one example of the great variety of living machines that adorn the planet. The eventuality of death is the great and silent motivator of human culture, spirituality and progress.

As Laura and her Dad sat like sentinels at the outpost of the dying, a strange and sweet tranquility

Awakening from a Distant Dream

descended upon them. Time seemed to hover above them instead of moving on. Long hours passed in which the air was filled with a presence that seemed to sweep all irrelevant thoughts aside. It was like daydreaming without content. Finally, it came. Ruth began to gasp for air. Her mouth stayed wide open and her nostrils flared, but to no avail. She took one final and desperate gulp of air, and let life pass from her. Ruth's face grew instantly calm and her features relaxed releasing all bodily tension. She was freed of pain at last. She was at peace, at last.

At that precise moment of dying, Edward gasped. He was frightened and confused. Laura looked over at him, got up, walked behind his chair and held him tightly. He collapsed in her arms and sobbed. His body shook with great heaving tremors. It was as if all the bottled feelings of a lifetime rose to the surface destined to be discharged within his daughter's embrace. Laura looked at him and saw her Daddy at last. It was one of those magical moments in life when the floodgates of true intuition open up and let out the truth. She understood that she needed to care for him. After a while, he got up, came over to his wife, placed his fingers on her eyelids and closed them. He held her hand, bent over her and kissed her tenderly on the cheek.

In the Grips of Pregnancy

Following her mother's burial, Laura stayed on with her Dad. In many ways, she became his surrogate wife and mother catering to his needs. She had become nearly completely domesticated. She took care of all the household chores, managed his finances and all the details that encompass daily life. These tasks managed to occupy all her waking hours. She often wondered to herself how she got into such a position - it was certainly not something she had planned on. What little time she had left, once the basic chores were done, was consumed by catering to her father's many physical needs. His health was steadily deteriorating. Ruth gave him cause to keep on living, and without her he was beginning to let go. He grew increasingly dependent on his daughter's presence. It was not long before Laura began to feel the drain on her own energy and resources. What was particularly alarming to her was the fact that her Dad had supplanted her mother's place at the television. It was now her father who sat within its mesmerizing and ghostly influence, hour after hour. He also began to show that particular pallor and characteristic deadness in the eyes so reminiscent of her mother. She realized that she could not go on this way for much longer. She wondered why she had not written to Matteo about Ruth's death. In some convoluted way, she felt responsible for these events and was afraid to acknowledge their existence.

One evening with her father fast asleep upstairs and the house wonderfully quiet, she sat down at her desk and began to write to Matteo, who was never very far from her thoughts. "Dearest One," she began, "I know it's been a long time, and I know I should have told you sooner, but my mother passed away. She had a terrible death. My father was devastated. I am now staying with him and

Awakening from a Distant Dream

helping him during this awful time. I know that you would approve. I miss you terribly. I hope to return as soon as I feel he has recovered enough to manage on his own. I trust that it will not be long.

"It is interesting how the influences of home reasserted themselves so quickly once I was here regardless of how much time has passed. It's almost as if the spirit of childhood has lingered in the house long after I left. Maybe it's the spirit of that child that fills me once I returned.

"I watched my mother die. I felt a tenderness in her at her death that I never felt when she was living. By the way, I must confess that one of the thoughts that was on my mind when it was happening was to capture the moment of death on canvas. As soon as I get back, that will be one of the things I plan to do. I hope everything is well with you. I Love you dearly, Laura."

Simply writing that letter filled Laura with both longing and relief. The moments that she had totally to herself - when she was not catering to her father - were punctuated by many thoughts and feelings. It was if she had an abundance of characters dancing in her head. At one moment, she was filled with a great melancholy and sense of loss over her mother. She blamed herself for treating the woman too harshly. The next moment, she felt angered and abused by both her parents. She thought of the life she might have had, had she been raised with greater love, compassion and understanding; this made her feel terribly cheated. She thought about her ambiguous feelings about men; thoughts of Paul and Danny plagued her. She remembered Paul's brutality and Danny's terrible indifference and cruelty. The vivid memory of Paul's attempted rape and Danny's abusive behavior left a residue of hurt and pain that would probably always be with her. But in spite of these feelings, she knew a place of comfort and relief. She reminded herself of the wonderful man who loved her. She had to discover, however, that place of security within her own being that did not require the support or adulation of others. Without it, there existed a void in her existence. This emptiness, in part, provided the fuel for the passion expressed through her art. The solitude she now experienced gave her an unmistakable opportunity to reflect on her inner self. She was able to look at her own tapestry of emotions, her own myriad confusions, and the many ambiguities that now paraded before her in the depths of her loneliness. She also had a vague suspicion that something was happening to her. Her body felt somehow different, but she did not know how. It was not as if she were ill; although, she did feel disconnected.

Now that his wife had died, Edward no longer had her to care for. The energy he had used to sustain his wife occupied nearly every breath of his existence and now he was infused with loneliness. Although they had shared no intimacy for years, he had grown inured to her presence, and in some remarkable way he had loved her. He never would have guessed how much he would miss her. Maybe it was because he was able to see the essence of the soul of the woman who had ravaged herself with alcohol. In his heart, he felt partly responsible for her decline. He could have, he thought, intervened and demanded something more of her. He could have asserted himself, especially on his daughter's behalf. He would never forgive himself for what he had allowed to happen to Laura, whom he loved with such abandon.

In his more lucid moments, he realized that he was waiting for death. He no longer was holding onto life. As a matter of fact, it had been a long time since he had looked forward to the unfolding of his own existence. He could easily trace that time to when Laura had no longer needed him or confided in him. He felt that his hand had been mostly dealt; he was at that point of giving up caring for himself entirely. The fact that he had to take care of Ruth was all that sustained him. Somehow Laura's presence in the house could not deter him from his course. He had spent too many years detached from human intimacy to be able to change at this point.

Laura was in the bathroom taking a shower. She was feeling nauseous. This had been happening to her a lot lately. When she got out of the shower, she looked at herself in the full-length mirror and noticed that her abdomen looked a little bloated. She placed these pieces of information side by side with the fact that she was quite late for her period. Suddenly, the reality of her condition sprang into her mind with a ferocious leap, "Oh my God," she sighed, "I'm pregnant!"

This conclusion was inescapable as soon as it was reached. It only needed to be confirmed by a doctor. Now Laura was faced with a terrible dilemma. The reality of her pregnancy brought to her consciousness a flood of feelings that resided in the very center of her female being. Surprisingly, she embraced the idea of a baby with unexpected delight. An avenue of existence had forged itself within her; an entirely new sense of self was beginning to awaken and emerge. The reality of her circumstances, however, brought with it many complicating issues.

When Laura got off the telephone with her doctor, she felt somewhat relieved but not surprised by the results; she was indeed pregnant. She felt terribly distressed for she was some thousands of miles and on the other side of the ocean from her lover, and she was now taking care of her father who was in rapidly declining health. Everything seemed to have worked against her and she felt terribly trapped by circumstance. Fate seemed to have dealt her a very cruel hand. The unfolding of events in an individual lifetime often have absolutely no regard for the person so affected – impaled as we are on the impervious arrow of time.

In the Grips of Pregnancy

Anxious about her future and uncertain about herself, Laura was plagued with sleepless nights. Assaulted as she was by exhaustion, her thoughts lost their usual clarity. She debated whether or not to have the baby. Her emotions were at war with her intellect. She reasoned to herself that it would probably be wise to have an abortion. That prospect, however, made her feel full of guilt and trepidation; for although, the fetus inside of her was, as of yet, not completely formed, she was already establishing an undeniable bond with it. She was just beginning to learn the power of this attachment and the extremely cohesive bond that inevitably develops between a mother and her offspring.

She wondered whether she should tell Matteo or not. Her thoughts were drawn to him, and she missed him terribly. She reasoned that if she decided to have an abortion, it would not be a good idea to inform him. She concluded that it would be terribly unfair and unwise for her to do so. On the other hand, if she were to bring the fetus to term, then he most certainly should know. There was also the matter of her Dad. She found her life terribly conflicted by clashing loyalties and an unbearable state of nearly incessant insomnia. Confusion and its corollary of indecision seemed to have become her watchwords.

After some weeks, Laura was still considering the possibility of an abortion. The arguments kept oscillating back and forth in her head. Logic told her one thing; her emotions told her something quite different indeed. Finally, she decided that no one must know, and that she would have it done. It seemed like the sensible thing to do.

She was sitting on the cold and horribly uncomfortable chair with her feet in the stirrups waiting for the doctor to arrive to begin the procedure. The walls all around the room were decorated with colorful travel posters of wondrously calm blue-water getaways in stark contradiction to Laura's state of mind and what she was actually facing. She could feel her heart beating rapidly in her chest. The room felt inextricably cold to her. Her senses were acutely aware of the life she carried. The longer she had to wait in that vulnerable position with her genitals exposed, the angrier she became.

"What am I doing here?" she asked herself. Her mind was racing in a kind of schizophrenic frenzy. "It's the right thing to do. But, what am I going to do with a baby! I wouldn't know where to begin. My career would be over, and where would I find the time? What about Matteo? It's his baby too; how could I tell him that I've aborted his baby? Would he really want the baby? Maybe I need to tell him first. What am I going to do?" These thoughts went around and around in her head without resolution. She was lost in the vortex of her own ever increasing anxiety.

In the midst of this confusion, the doctor finally arrived. He came in showing all his teeth in a huge and highly implausible smile. His white hospital coat was meticulous. His vacuous hospital manner ripped at the open wound of Laura's sensibilities. "Hello, Laura," he said, as he extended his hand. "Have you been advised of the procedure?"

"Yes," she answered nervously.

"Good! Don't worry it's all quite routine. You'll be out of the clinic in about an hour."

The doctor put his plastic gloves on with a classic professional indifference to Laura's vulnerable position. He sat down and moved his chair so that his eyes were totally in line and fixated on Laura's vagina. His appreciation of her sex was purely clinical in nature.

Everything about the experience made Laura unbearably ill. The environment was so aseptic and devoid of feeling that she felt horribly humiliated. Feeling the cold gloved hand inside of her, shot through her consciousness. His touch was awkward and insensitive. She felt terribly humiliated; in fact, she felt violated. Laura suddenly rebelled against the experience that defined her present moment. She was about to leave a terrain that she found unbearable; She was about to cross her Rubicon. She ultimately surrendered to an inner voice that would not be silenced, and removed her feet from the stirrups and swung her legs around until they were near the floor. She stepped down. "I'm sorry, doctor; I've changed my mind."

"Are you sure?" he asked, startled by this sudden and abrupt decision.

"Yes, yes, I'm very sure I can't do this."

"Very well then," he replied, removing his gloves and making no effort to disguise his annoyance; he left the room. The fact that he made no attempt to offer comfort to her under such a set of circumstances, convinced her all the more that she had made the right decision.

After she got dressed and walked out of the clinic, she sighed. It was a sigh full of profound relief. She was inexplicably happy. The day seemed somehow more vibrant and alive than it was when she had first gone to the clinic. She had lifted a great weight from herself, and felt more alive for it.

Of course, she was now faced with the monumental task of ordering her life around this new life that was burgeoning inside of her. Along with this decision came a whole galaxy of complicating issues that would certainly pursue her. Surely, she would now have to tell Matteo of her pregnancy, or maybe it might be better to remove herself from his life altogether. These opposing ideas and conclusions danced in her head like bickering and demented genies. No matter what scenarios she envisioned, the presence of her father was always there. She had an inescapable responsibility to him, from that she did not waver.

One evening while her Dad was on the couch staring at the flickering from the television, she sat down beside him. "Dad," she began, "I have to talk to you."

Awakening from a Distant Dream

He turned his head listlessly towards her, "Yes Laura, what is it?"

"I need to turn off the television," and she got up to turn off the set. She returned to him and continued, "I'm going to have a baby."

His expression quickly changed from a blank and distant stare to one of surprise and shock; it was as if he was suddenly awakened from a deep sleep. "You're pregnant," he said as if turning the idea around in his mind to examine its veracity. He remained silent for a time, and then he spoke, "How wonderful! I am happy for you. It's amazing; I'm going to be a grandfather. Oh my gosh!"

His reaction, totally caught Laura off guard. She was expecting to be judged by him; she was anticipating the necessity to defend herself. She was sure he would ask her all kinds of questions about the father, and be critical about her situation. It made her realize how little she knew the man.

She could not restrain herself; she threw her arms around him. "Dad, I love you," she said. "Don't you want to know about the father?"

"You can tell me whatever you want, whenever you want to."

"Thank you," she answered. She looked at him closely and could see that he suddenly seemed exhausted. She got up and turned the television back on. He reflexively turned his head towards the screen, and seemed to slide back into a passive state of being – one that provided him considerable solace. She quietly left him there in the room immersed as he was in his internal reflections.

The Pain of Separation

Matteo found it very difficult to sleep. His nights were tormented by thoughts of Laura. He missed her kindness, her warmth, her softness and delicacy. Somehow, receiving her letter intensified these feelings rather than easing his general state of anxiety. He chided himself for these feelings. They were not reasonable for a man of his age, he tried to tell himself. But reason had no place among such powerful emotions that were so obviously a consequence of the love he felt for her.

The concentration he usually devoted to his work suffered as a result of his intense longing. He would not admit to himself that he was terribly hurt. Was there anything that she was not telling him? Was there another reason for her leaving other than what she said? These thoughts plummeted his mind into a kind of unsettling chaos that was all too reminiscent of youth, yet was much harder for his more aging body to tolerate. His health was being adversely affected.

As day followed day with still no further word from her, he felt a gnawing pain in his gut that would not subside. The discomfort ultimately forced him to visit his doctor.

"Matteo," the doctor said as his patient was putting on his shirt, "I think there's a chance that you're getting an ulcer. You seem agitated. It's unlike you. Is there a problem you want to talk about?"

"No, nothing Henri, nothing."

Matteo's reaction to the question was more than enough evidence to the contrary. "Come on," Henri insisted as he removed his glasses temporarily to clean them, "I've known you long enough. What's the problem?"

Matteo looked at his doctor and saw the sincerity and concern in his eyes. He was put at emotional ease by

Awakening from a Distant Dream

Henri's rounded and kindly face. Henri was Matteo's doctor and friend. He smiled, "All right, Laura went to America to be with her dying mother, or so she told me. Her mother passed away, but now it seems her father is ill. She wrote to me, so at least I know she is all right. Lately, I have heard nothing. Sometimes I think that there are things she is not telling me. I never suspected how much I would miss her. I'm very worried about her, yet I'm not sure I want to know the whole truth. To be honest, it's driving me crazy."

"It's love then as I suspected. Why don't you call or write to her?"

"No, I cannot. I'm an old man; she is young. I will not pressure her. If she is to come back to me, it must be her own desire to do so, and only when she is ready. Do you understand?"

"Well I know that if you are an old man you are a foolish one," the doctor answered and smiled broadly at his patient. "You need to take care of yourself. I'm going to prescribe some medicine for your stomach, and please, watch your diet. At our age, we need to pay attention to these things. Take care of yourself!"

"I will and thank you for listening. Addio."

"Addio."

As the days wore on without further word from Laura, his worst fears seemed to be verified. She left him, he reasoned. He did not blame her. He was legitimately interested in her happiness. He did feel, however, that her art would suffer on account of the separation. He felt that she was not prepared as of yet to go off on her own career. He felt that too many facets of her artistic persona and her artistic education remained unfinished. He knew how important the proper development of the craft was in the life of an artist, especially at the beginning of the journey.

Beginnings and Endings

As she lay there in the birthing room, well-lit and cheerfully decorated, she could feel her acutely profound apprehension growing more pervasive. She found herself on the verge of giving birth for the first time in her life, but was facing it desperately alone. She was at a loss as to know what to expect, and, more importantly, how she would behave. The outcome, she knew, was dependent on her own emotional and physical reactions to the experience. As the time grew closer, she felt more and more terrified. The nurse on call, Sarah, a dark-eyed young woman with an olive complexion and almost moon-shaped face, recognized the state that she was in. Sarah was endowed with a remarkable ability to understand and empathize with her patients.

"Laura," she said, "let's see how you're doing." She then proceeded to delicately examine Laura's cervix. "Four centimeters," she said, "your birth is progressing well. I don't think it will be too much longer." She took some ice and placed it in Laura's mouth, "Does that feel better?" she asked. Laura nodded. "Good, now don't worry; everything will be fine. Is there anyone here with you?"

"No," Laura said emphatically. Sarah immediately understood the cause of Laura's distress.

"I'll tell you what, I'll stay with you as much as I can, all right."

"Thank you," Laura responded.

Laura was not prepared for the intense pain that came with her contractions as her cervix was widening itself and the uterus was preparing to expel its transient hostage. She yelled out in a kind of agonized fury. In the midst of this suffering, she despised Matteo and herself for bringing all this on. "Damn him," she yelled out. "How did I get myself into this situation? What's the matter with me? Here I am all alone giving birth; I could die right on this bed. I should have gotten the abortion." The physical torment seemed like it would never end. The pain came in waves and with each succeeding contraction, the pain grew more intense. She had never known pain like she was experiencing. Sarah remained by her side and tried her best to encourage her. She placed a cool wet towel on Laura's forehead, and applied gentle massage to her body. When she was dilated to ten centimeters, Sarah summoned the doctor.

As the doctor was sitting at the portal of her being, he attempted to reassure her. "Keep up with the breathing; you're doing fine. I know you'll feel like pushing, but don't push until I tell you." Laura was completely caught up in her own feelings, yet the mere sound of his voice was reassuring. Just when Laura reached the point where she felt she could no longer bear the intensity of the pain, the doctor said, "All right Laura, start pushing." The baby soon emerged.

Following the birth, he lifted the baby and showed it to Laura and said, "It's a healthy boy. You should feel proud of yourself." He carefully placed the baby on Laura's stomach with the chord still attached. While she was looking into her baby's eyes, she felt her heart give itself totally to him. The doctor cut the cord and then placed the baby higher on Laura's abdomen. "You could hold him now if you want before we'll have to examine him more carefully. I wouldn't worry - he looks very healthy; it's routine hospital policy."

As soon as Laura took the baby in her arms, she was lost within the exquisite and uncompromising love of a mother for her child. It is the kind of love that could easily lead her to give up her own life for the baby's welfare if that was called for. It's the kind of love that has ensured the survival of the species in spite of its own tendency towards self-destruction. It's the power of such love that radically altered Laura's life at that moment.

Beginnings and Endings

Sarah looked on as Laura was lost within this singular connection that irrevocably ties a mother to her child. She asked Laura, "Do you have a name for him?" Laura looked up, startled by the intrusion of another voice, "No, I really haven't given it a thought." Quite suddenly a name came to her. "What do you think of Michael?"

"That's a beautiful name. I like it."

"Michael," Laura said as she looked at the infant immersed in the warmth and nurture of his mother. After a while both mother and baby fell asleep. Sarah carefully undid Laura's hold on the child and lifted young Michael and handed him to the nurse that would give Michael his first experience with distress outside the womb. His toe was stuck with a needle to draw blood. He was prodded and poked and examined in the smallest detail.

Since both mother and child were deemed perfectly healthy, it was not long before they were both ready to go home. She was looking forward to bringing Michael home and showing him to her father. Edward felt badly that he couldn't come with Laura to the hospital, but was thrilled with the prospect of seeing his grandchild – an opportunity he would never have imagined to be possible in his lifetime.

After she had said her good-byes to Sarah and the doctor, she got into a cab with her new charge and went home. On the way, she bemused herself with the thought that she would be taking care of two beings, one just born and the other nearing death. These responsibilities came upon her quickly, giving her little time to adjust to her new set of circumstances. Laura had no real experience dealing with the needs of humans at the beginning or near the end of life. She faced a seemingly impossible situation, yet she did not fully comprehend the remarkable resiliency of the human spirit.

Awakening from a Distant Dream

There was literally no time in the day for her to take care of her own needs. The demands that both her little infant and her father constantly placed upon her tested her capacity for caring and physical endurance. To make this burden seem exceedingly worse, she had no friends or companions to confide in or in whom she could take solace. Her existence seemed to be overtaken and ravaged by the needs of others.

She realized, even with the best of intentions, that this could not go on for long before she would inevitably fracture under the sheer weight of it all. Her sleep became fitful and was usually interrupted by the baby. During those brief moments that were truly her own, she tried not to feel sorry for herself. She desperately tried to avoid thinking about Matteo, since such thoughts would magnify her pain. Pride and guilt were co-conspirators keeping her from contacting him. The ocean that separated them seemed too broad to fathom. She wished to keep her mind on a sense of higher purpose, but she was aching inside. She desperately needed to hear the understanding voice of another human and feel the warmth of compassion and good humor. She cried out from her inner soul for a friend.

Sometimes, despite her best efforts, when she looked down and saw her baby at her breast and felt the radiance and purity of his innocence, she would be reminded of the man who loved her and gave her this baby. "Matteo," she would whisper to herself, "I'm sorry!" She knew that it was her own stubbornness that kept her so far away from her lover. Laura understood, at such moments, how she could be her own worst enemy, but yet she felt that she did not have much choice given the circumstances she found herself in. She could have called out for help, but she was in such an exhausted and confused state of mind. It was not confusion she sought, but clarity. That clarity of thought and vision is the fervent secret wish of every artist who chooses to take whatever path the pursuit of art might suggest. It was Matteo who constantly reminded her of that and encouraged her to never allow the flame to die. But now there was no time for art; her creative spirit had been crowded out by the relentless details of living that needed immediate attention. "Michael," she whispered to herself, "forgive your poor mother!" The rush of tears that came with these feelings fell on the infant's tender face. He stirred only briefly, too intent on getting nurture. Laura was operating on meager resources and the sense of hopelessness she was beginning to feel was further magnified by her exhaustion. She thought she could not handle any additional disruption in her life.

While all of these changes were taking place inside of her, her father was slowly and painfully in decline. His moments of lucidity were rapidly diminishing over time. During those occasions when he was more himself, he enjoyed the company of his grandchild, but they were of short duration. Most of the time, he remained aloof and withdrawn, and when he did speak it seemed shrill and demanding. As is often the case with the elderly, he frequently felt disoriented and confused; this state of mind resulted in feelings of angst, frustration and anger. Edward was frightened, for he knew that he was nearing the end of his sojourn. Though this increasingly taxed Laura's energy and patience already in a precarious state, she was painfully aware of her father's worsening condition.

Edward awoke every morning with a severe headache that became more severe as the day progressed. He refused to go see a doctor about his condition in spite of Laura's repeated insistence. This went on for months; although, he had told his daughter that the headaches had stopped. He knew that something was seriously wrong with him, but he had lost all desire to take care of himself and really wished to die.

Awakening from a Distant Dream

One afternoon, Laura was playing with her baby in the front room of the house. They were both lost in that wonderful world of unadulterated joyfulness that only children can engender. She was without a care - totally involved in the present. Suddenly, her attention was shattered by a dull thud that came from upstairs. She sensed that something was wrong. She placed the baby in his playpen; he immediately began to cry feeling his mother's distress.

Laura ran up the stairs shouting, "Dad, Dad are you all right?" There was no answer. She ran to his room and opened the door; it was empty. She looked down the hallway and rushed to the bathroom. Her heart was beating rapidly in her chest. Beads of perspiration formed on her forehead. She opened the door slowly. There on the floor was her Dad, his face pressed hard against the bathroom tiles and his pants still gathered around his feet. He did not seem to be moving. She went over to him, knelt by his head and started to shake him at his shoulders hoping that he might awaken. He did not move. She grabbed at his pants by the belt loops and with great effort pulled them above his hips. She then pushed his heavy body onto his side and placed her hand on his jugular trying to feel for a pulse. There was none. She watched for any sign of movement or breathing. He was certainly dead.

All her strength, all her emotional reserves drained from her as if the core of her being had been violated. She collapsed onto the body of her father and felt numb. A great sorrow enveloped her, but even in the midst of this her artist's spirit captured the irony of this scene. She was physically closer to the body of her dead father than she ever had been to him when he was alive. How desperately alone she felt at that moment.

The funeral was a lonely affair. The room where his body was placed had rows of folding chairs, all empty. After two days, there was not a single name on the guest book. It was a testimonial to her father's solitary and morose existence. Apart from his wife and daughter, he had no one. Laura imagined that what really had killed him was the fact that he ate himself up from the inside. Just a year had separated the deaths of her parents. Now that they were gone, she realized how little she had known of them and their inner lives, their internal fears, their anguish and even their joys. They had been a great mystery to her. Now she felt not so much regret, but a deep sense of loss.

Laura now found herself alone in the large house with her child. Her solitude seemed to have become greatly magnified. She became fearful of the night, being alone as she was. The sensitivity and imagination that she so depended on as an artist heightened her attention to the details of her environment. The smallest things would frighten her - the push of the wind against the old window frames, the sound of neighborhood cats fighting, the shrill and unsettling sound of a passing ambulance and sometimes her own breathing. Gradually, this general apprehension began to deprive her of sleep. Eventually, she became dependent upon tranquilizers to get her through the night. The benefit of even these medications soon wore off.

Finally, she went to see her doctor. "Doctor," she said, "the tranquilizers don't seem to be helping anymore, what should I do?"

Doctor Dorland was middle-aged, tall and thin with small unexpressive eyes that were magnified into absurd proportions by thick rimmed eyeglasses. He was nervous by temperament and constantly moved around in his seat. His hair was in disarray. He gave Laura the impression that he was perpetually distracted. "I'm not surprised," he answered. "You need a change. You need a rest. You have to get away from that house at least for a while. I recommend you go on a trip somewhere, take a vacation. Do you have any friends or family that you can visit?"

Awakening from a Distant Dream

"Yes, possibly," she answered although that was a lie, for she did not have the resources or the inclination to travel.

"Good," he said. "That's what I recommend you do."

The entire interview lasted a few minutes. "Some advice," she said to herself after leaving his office. "What am I going to do for money? What am I going to do with the baby?" A deep depression began its assault on her once again. She saw no way out of this loneliness – despair seemed to be taking hold of her. She had forgotten her art; she had forgotten her lover's admonitions. She looked into the future and saw a level plateau as far as the eye could see without any respite from the monotonous and unappealing terrain. She felt that she had truly failed at living.

Matteo woke up suddenly from sleep. He felt agitated and was filled with a formidable sense of dread. Immediately, he thought of Laura. He sensed that she needed him, but he felt entirely helpless. He longed for her and wanted her, yet he did not know how to bridge the physical and emotional distance between them. He finally decided to seek some advice from his dear friend, Francesca, a sculptress. She lived in her studio. It was an open space filled with light that was strangely amplified by her plaster and stone creations. As a sculptress, Francesca had the remarkable ability to capture her figures in motion.

As soon as Matteo came into the studio, his mood instantly lightened. Her current project was of a woman marathon runner. Although unfinished, Matteo marveled at the way Francesca showed the dynamic tension of the runner's body and a ferocious determination embodied in her facial expressions. It was as if the stone was coming to life. As she was working on the piece, she seemed to dance around it. Her motions were graceful and precise as she was deftly placing her chisel on the, as yet unfinished, right foot and striking meticulous blows with her mallet. Periodically, she would stop working, step back and circle the figure with her long artist's apron swaying with her movements. The sculptress and her creation looked like lovers bathed in sunlight streaming in from the overhead skylight. Francesca was immediately aware of his presence but continued working. He was awed by her power of creation.

"I'm sorry to disturb you," he said.

"Nonsense," was her reply. They greeted each other with a kiss. She stepped away from the figure, looked at it admiringly and put down her tools. She was well aware of Matteo's situation, and often took on the role of his confidant.

"Francesca, it's breathtaking!" he said.

"Do you really think so?" she asked.

"I wouldn't tell you if I thought otherwise. You know that."

"Well then, I'm pleased. What brings you here my dear friend?" she asked.

"To see you, of course," he answered.

"Come on, out with it!"

What Matteo loved so much about his friend was her uncanny straightforwardness. "I can tell by looking at you that you are troubled. Talk to me. Come, let's sit down," she said as she led him by the hand to the couch next to the window overlooking a sumptuous garden in the front room. The room was bright and airy. She had adorned it with beautiful yet simple decorations. There were plants everywhere adding to an overwhelming sense of lightness where dark thoughts had no place to find nurture. This atmosphere had helped Matteo feel at ease with himself, and made it easier for him to open his heart to his dear friend.

"You are too perceptive. Last time we talked, I told you how Laura had to go the States to take care of her mother. Well, she has written to me a few times, but has recently stopped writing. I'm a little concerned about her, but, more than that, I miss her. There is something she is not telling me. I don't think she will come back to me. I thought I could accept that possibility, but I feel lost without her. I thought I was too old to feel these things again. Francesca, what should I do; I feel so helpless?"

"Go find her, of course!"

"I can't do that; I can't interfere, besides, I'm not even sure of where she lives. I wouldn't know even where to begin to look for her."

"Matteo, you can be such a fool. Are you trying to tell me that a grown and sophisticated man like yourself could be so incapable of figuring all that out! It seems to me that you prefer to suffer, or perhaps you're afraid?"

He looked at her for a moment and thought. She had said something that resonated strongly with something deep within. "Afraid," he replied, "yes, that's possible. Maybe I am afraid to find out what has happened to her. Maybe she doesn't need me anymore. Maybe she found someone else, someone younger. After all, she is so much younger than I."

"You always manage to amaze me. Sure you're older than she is, but she loves you. Go to her. Find out where she is and go to her. You have friends over at the American Embassy don't you?"

"Yes, yes of course," he replied.

"Well then, go to them and ask them for help. What do you have to lose?"

Matteo gazed at his friend thoughtfully. "You're right, as usual. I will go to her. Anything is better than this awful state I'm in. Anyway, enough about myself, how have you been?"

"Well, I have my work, and, for right now, that's more than enough. I've been commissioned to create a whole series for the International Games. I have barely enough time to finish or eat and sleep for that matter."

Beginnings and Endings

"I'm looking forward to seeing them all when you're done."

"I'll certainly let you know and give you a private showing. Now leave me! My runner awaits me."

Matteo stood up; he could feel Francesca's impatience. "You're right; it's about time I got going. Thanks so much for listening to me, as usual."

She kissed him gently on the cheek, "My pleasure, you have always been a dear friend to me. Now don't waiver and go find your love. If you don't you'll regret it, and, besides, you'll have to listen to me."

No Stranger at Her Door

Laura was in the middle of a very fitful sleep when she heard a knocking at her door. "I wonder who that could be?" she thought. She shouted in a very irritated voice as she got up, "Who is it? Do you realize how late it is!" There was no answer. She looked through the little peep hole. Her heart momentarily stopped beating as she saw Matteo's face framed in the tiny aperture. The displeasure that she initially felt when she was awakened instantly evaporated. She hurriedly opened the door. They looked at each other for the longest moment - their hearts floating blissfully above their heads. They embraced with the energy of a long-suppressed passion breaking through the thin veneer of control.

"Oh Matteo!" she sighed. "How I have missed you." Matteo was speechless, he held on to her with a feeling of absolute joy permeating his being.

"How did you find me?" she finally asked.

"I had your letter. Some friends of mine at the American Embassy helped me to locate you even though you did not leave a forwarding address. It took them awhile; they do have their methods. They were also kind enough to help me plan the trip. I would have been truly helpless without them. This country of yours is very grand and so terribly large; it would be so easy to get lost. I took a bus from New York to Chicago. Amazing, I have never spent so many hours on a bus before. I had no idea what a big country America is.

"Why did you take so long to write me and why did you stop? Why the secrecy? I was convinced that you were not telling me everything. I was afraid you had grown tired of me and were seeing someone else. My pride was preventing me from coming to you; until, a friend of mine, smarter than I, told me how foolish I was being."

No Stranger at Her Door

"I am thankful to your friend and so glad that your pride did not win out," Laura answered. "At first, I thought it would be unfair of me to burden you with my problems. After that it was just harder and harder to break free of my own isolation. Matteo, how I have missed you! I've missed the comfort of your arms and the way you talk to me. I've missed the way you listen to me. There is no one that could ever replace you.

"It's so good to see your kind, sweet face again. But you know, many times when I felt deeply in trouble, I would picture your face in my mind and it was a great comfort to me. You have been my salvation even though you were so far away."

Laura fell silent and as soon as she did, the hunger of their bodies took control. She led him into her bedroom. They undressed each other. She, however, noticed his hesitation, and when she looked carefully at him she could see that he had no erection.

"What's the matter?" she asked.

He sighed noticeably, "I don't know. It's been so long. I don't think my body has caught up with my emotions. Maybe, I'm upset with you for staying away so long. It was very hard for me." He said this without malice. He said it reluctantly because his body would not let him hide it; such is the nature of intimacy.

"I'm sorry," Laura said, kissing him tenderly on the cheek. "I needed to find myself again. My mother's death brought up so many issues I had to face head on. I had to take care of my father, and what made matters far worse was that he passed away soon after." At this point she decided it was the wrong time to tell him about the birth of his son. "Can you understand?" she asked.

"Well, yes and no. I understand feelings of confusion and doubt; I know them well, but why couldn't you at least let me know what you were dealing with and that you were all right? I am so sorry that you lost both of your parents so close together. I somehow knew that you were keeping things from me. I would have hoped that you trusted me enough to share all this. I worried about you; I needed to know that you were safe."

"You're right, I'm sorry. Can you forgive me?"

She said this with such tenderness reflected in her loving eyes that Matteo became aroused by the power of her affection. He mounted and penetrated her sweetness. The love they made together that night was filled with the textures of many feelings - the exquisite happiness of being reunited, the poignancy of being so long separated, the joy of intimacy. This filled both their cups that had been empty for so long.

Very early the next morning, they were awakened by the unmistakable cries of an infant.

"What is that?" he asked.

Laura looked at him with such loving intensity that he already knew the answer.

"That is your son, Michael!"

"Michele, my son. Michele."

"I was reluctant to tell you. I know how stupid that was. I was afraid that you would not want him. I tried to get an abortion. I just couldn't."

Matteo was in shock; he just kept muttering, "My son, my son." Having heard that he had a son greeted him with such powerful emotions that he did not hear anything else she was saying. Then he looked up at Laura and said, very simply, "I love you!"

"You're not angry with me?"

"Angry with you, no, never. Let me see him!"

She went into the bedroom and returned with little Michael cradled in her arms. She rocked him gently. She then handed the infant to his father.

He held the young baby with extreme and unabated tenderness. Tears were cascading from his eyes, "I am sorry that I was not here to help you. I'm sorry."

No Stranger at Her Door

She went over to him and encircled both him and the baby with her arms. It was a moment of exquisite joy – the kind of experience whose memory would not be extinguished until death.

Later that day, Matteo finally told her when he felt the time was right, "Laura, I want to take you and Michele back with me to Paris where we belong, and I want us to live together." To his astonishment, she quickly accepted his invitation.

Return to the City of Eternal Light

Laura was quite surprised at how quickly she rediscovered her city.   The exuberance of her feelings clearly demonstrated to her how she belonged there and, in some ways, had never really left.   Along with these rediscovered feelings, came the re-emergence of her artist's soul. It had the effect on her that Matteo had hoped for.

It was not long before she was painting again. The subject of her work had become something that was intimate to her, Michael. Her paintings attempted to reflect not only the physical dimension but also the emotional and spiritual dimensions of a growing human child.   They found an apartment together and it soon became cluttered with sketches having this unifying thread as its theme. That first year back in Paris with Matteo had a magical and ethereal quality that she would never forget. She was light and playful with life. Life became for her like a river, ever moving, changeable and exuberant.   It had a wonderful clarity about it that she thoroughly embraced.

They were both happy in their hearts, and life for them had become a wonderful dance.   They laughed, played and loved with abandon.   Their child benefited greatly from this interaction between his parents.   He absorbed the intense emotions and seemed to thrive in their embrace.   Many years later, as a young man, Michael would often reflect on the delight of those times. Whenever he looked at those paintings of himself as a young boy they would recapture the vortex of wondrous feelings that surrounded them.

Matteo continued his teaching.   The onerous lethargy and boredom that he felt during Laura's absence was quickly replaced with a renewed energy. He now had a family to take care of. Whenever he looked at this son, he was amazed at the fact that he had a child so late in life. Rather than being frightened by this reality, he considered himself very fortunate. He hoped that his health would sustain him and that he would have the opportunity to see the young child become a man. In fact, his thoughts were often filled with images of Michael as an adult. He could not only visualize his features but also see his persona. He was convinced that his son was destined for great things – it is every parent's wishful dream. What form Michael's accomplishments would take was, of course, unknown to him. Realistically, Matteo did not see himself as having any special psychic powers. These images came not from his soul but rather his heart.

One morning, he was inspired to give these images tangible and undeniable form. He took to creating a sculpture of the young man that he imagined to be the essence of his son. He poured such passion into the clay that the sculpture started to take on a kind of life of its own. Matteo worked with an amazing focus and drive that even surprised him. Everything else around him merged into a kind of annoying background. In the midst of this seemingly boundless artistic fervor, he even ignored Laura. She, an artist herself, however, did not take offense and sought to make sure he was interrupted as little as possible so he could concentrate entirely on his work. After all, it was something that he had done for her many times.

One evening, he had come to bed out of sheer exhaustion. Laura happened to still be awake. He was very restless. She extended her hand and gently stroked his forehead.

"How is it coming?" she asked.

"I don't know," he answered. "Tonight it seemed hopelessly flawed. I was so tired that if I continued I knew I would surely ruin it." He suddenly grew quiet and began to sob.

"What's the matter?" Laura asked.

"I love that young boy so. I just hope that I deserve him and you."

Awakening from a Distant Dream

The simplicity and beauty of what he had said made her feel like her heart was about to melt within her.

"Oh Matteo," she sighed and laid her hand across his chest. It was that sensitivity and childlike openness that Laura so dearly loved. A smile came across her face when Laura realized that he had fallen asleep. It was as if, with his soul so unburdened, he was able to surrender completely to sleep. Their lives proceeded on this course during the early years of Michael's upbringing. The young boy grew and thrived among such enriched surroundings.

Beneath this happiness that they both obviously shared, however, there were layers of feelings that were not quite as sanguine. Laura and Matteo were both complex personalities. They constantly struggled throughout life to find meaning from the often haphazard nature of experience. They both demanded clarity often where none existed. Beneath the ceaseless demands of living, resided many unanswered questions. With a family to raise, the solitude that was necessary to examine oneself deeply was difficult, if not impossible, to come by.

Although they both tried to give each other enough room to be by themselves with their own thoughts and a space where their creativities could thrive, the needs of a child often disrupted this unspoken agreement. They were both under a considerable amount of stress, for a child's demands are necessarily relentless. Little Michael did not see them as autonomous creatures but rather as parents who were there to meet his needs for love and protection. The world they were immersed in as parents was quite normal, yet they were unprepared for it. Given this new reality, it became quite common for Matteo and Laura to take issue with each other over who was to take care of the boy. Matteo was growing less and less patient with his familial responsibilities due in large part to his age. He no longer had the kind of energy and stamina that is required in parenting. These disagreements between them were not trivial and eventually worked their way insidiously into the bedroom.

"I'm sorry, Matteo," Laura said in a barely audible voice. "I'm just too tired."

He was completely aroused. An intense anger welled up within him. He understood, however, that this intense emotion came from his sexual frustration. He tried to keep his feelings in check. Another and far more important reason for his reluctance to express his anger was the nagging fear that if he pressed the issue, Laura might say things that would be critical of his capacity as a lover. Again, the fact of their age difference plagued him, and it grew worse the older he became.

"It's all right," he finally answered. "You should get your rest."

"Thank you, but what about you?" she asked as her hand found his erection.

He moved away from her touch. "I'm fine," he answered with a bit of an edge in his tone. She could not help but feel his distress. She could not help but feel guilty, for it was not tiredness that dissuaded her from making love but an alarming lack of desire.

Sexual passion began to suffer. This cooling grew more severe over time. Neither clearly understood why this was so. Secretly, Matteo feared that Laura's lack of interest was because he had become unattractive to her. Laura felt, for her part, that it was her fault, that it was her prolonged absence from Matteo that was at the heart of the change.

There is such a delicate balance of feelings, emotions and desire that fuels and maintains the intimacy between humans, that anything that disturbs the intricate dance can jeopardize the relationship. It is as if the complex structure of a house is delicately pivoted upon a narrow beam and its uprightness is dependent upon the precise distribution of weight inside. There is a critical

Awakening from a Distant Dream

mass that if moved from off-center can result in the collapse of the entire structure.

For Laura and Matteo, that critical mass was being reached, and either they did not know what to do about it, or they were unable to act on their perceptions. Paradoxically, in this case, it seemed that both were true.

It was a spectacular summer evening. Twilight was dancing across the face of Paris. The full moon was rising and appeared large and voracious enough to consume the entire city. Laura was at her easel but was unable to concentrate, not so much because of the moon's dominance, but because of its ability to pull a very dark mood out of her into consciousness.

She was feeling a hunger inside of her. It was a hunger that even art was unable to satisfy. As she looked at the canvas in front of her, it seemed strangely empty and flat. On it she had tried to create a portrait of her son. Although it was technically good, it failed to evoke any kind of emotion. Suddenly, she filled her broad brush with azure blue and smeared the paint across the canvas with rapid and bold strokes. She then took the canvas and threw it against the wall leaving a streak of color as it fell to the floor. Where this urge to destroy came from she had no idea; although, she was not unfamiliar with its expression. In some ways it scared her.

She dropped the brush and literally collapsed into a seated position on the floor. Moonlight streamed through the window and cast deep shadows on her form, creating a macabre image. Her shoulders slumped in submission to the dark mood that now dominated her. Her face buried itself into her awaiting hands and she began to sob uncontrollably. This went on for some time with her emotions ebbing and flowing to their own rhythms. Composure finally did come to her only after she was entirely drained of energy. It was only then that she could begin to think constructively about her state of being.

Return to the City of Eternal Light

She felt unsettled and needed to know why. Matteo was not the reason and had never given her any cause for concern. Quite to the contrary, he was immensely supportive of her and was always willing to listen and was receptive to her concerns no matter how seemingly trivial. She had no doubt that she loved Matteo and loved him deeply. Then why, she asked herself, did she feel so unsatisfied? Was it the sex? The sex was not as good as it once was, but she knew that it was not the cause but the effect. In the past she could project her dissatisfaction onto her partners like Marcel and feel perfectly justified. But, with Matteo this was not possible. Laura eventually came to the realization that the source of these feelings rested wholly within her. She was determined to discover the cause of her unhappiness.

Laura struggled with her feelings for a long time. She kept resurrecting the same thoughts over and over again. It was getting her nowhere. She understood, however, that things could no longer go on as they had been. Maybe what she needed was to get away for a little while in order to change her surroundings. Possibly such a change would help give her an entirely different perspective. "How would Matteo take to such an idea?" she wondered. Rather than act on these feelings, she buried them inside herself and was reluctant to think such thoughts again, for they threatened to harm all the relationships that she had come to depend upon for sustenance. Not surprisingly, this strategy was bound to fail.

Laura somehow managed to carve out some time for herself to devote to her work - in this case a linoleum block that she was struggling with. Matteo came in interrupting her and asked, "Laura have you seen Michael's blue jacket?"

Laura looked up at him with intensely piercing eyes, "I don't know where his damn jacket is! Why do you have to barge in on me like this! Can't you see that I'm working! Just go find it yourself and leave me alone!"

Matteo was completely taken aback by Laura's apparently inexplicable anger. He could not understand what had driven her to such an extreme emotion. He felt provoked and wanted to strike back at her, but he chose discretion instead. Without saying a word, he left the room, but not without showing by his expression that he was both angry and humiliated.

As soon as he left, Laura was overcome by her own emotions. She felt so inept and utterly stupid. It hurt her to feel that she had behaved so badly. She knew that he was not the problem. "What's the matter with me?" she asked herself. The answer was not forthcoming. The only thing she could conclude was that she needed to get away at least for a little while. Although this idea had passed through her mind before, this time she was not frightened by the thought or its implications; she was determined to make it happen. She could no longer abide the way she was feeling, and had to change her situation. She realized that Matteo would probably not understand, but she had made up her mind.

"Matteo," Laura said, as they were having breakfast, "I'm sorry about yesterday; I know I hurt you. Will you forgive me?"

"Of course," he replied. "But something must be wrong. It's not like you to act like that. I've never seen you so angry. Is everything all right?" Matteo often found women completely mystifying, but he did have enough experience with them to know that when a woman became explosive it was an indicator of a deeply felt and profound feeling usually related to matters of the heart. Unlike the male animal who is not reluctant to caste his anger about him like a dangerous weapon, a woman has to overcome an innate urge towards compassion and nurture before striking out.

Return to the City of Eternal Light

"Matteo," she began. She always took such great care when she pronounced his name and this time was no different. "I honestly don't know. I've just been feeling so unsatisfied and unhappy."

"I know," he said and his eyes brilliantly illustrated the depth of his empathy and his sadness.

Her hand reached out to his. He could feel her trembling. Matteo was tempted to say more, but no words came out of him. In some sense, he was afraid to know more realizing how even the simplest words could change things, so fragile is the hold we have on ourselves and others.

"I love you like I've never loved another. But, something isn't right with me. I know it has nothing to do with you. You treat me so well and really understand me in a way that often scares me. But, I feel so bound up - a prisoner in my own skin. Sometimes I feel that I can hardly breathe." On speaking the truth, her whole being felt lighter, but the pain was excruciating. She continued, "I have been so filled with anguish that I find it hard to work anymore. I'm so sorry!" With that, she fell into his arms.

Matteo held her and said, "There's no need to be sorry. I'm sorry that you've been in so much pain and that I've not even noticed. But I do understand. What can I do to help?" Matteo was often surprised by his own magnanimity. His years had taught him well. He had learned how destructive violent passion can be without the calming influence of humility and how dangerous emotions are when not counterbalanced by the mind's capacity for reason. He had known moments of pure integrity in his lifetime. This was one of those moments.

"You're not making this any easier for me," she said.

"I don't understand; what do you mean?" he asked with a little panic evident in his voice.

Awakening from a Distant Dream

"I think we need to separate for a little while; I need to get away and be on my own for a time so that I can make sense of all these feelings. I need to find clarity."

What he imagined to be the worst possible outcome had come to pass. He went into a state of shock. He felt numb and an overwhelming feeling of unreality usurped his senses. It took long and excruciating moments before he could summon up enough concentration to say, "Where would you go? What would you do?"

"I don't know. I need to find a place where I can take Michael and have the kind of peace I need to continue my work. I don't know how I will do this; I only know that it's something that I must do." She paused and could not help but see the shadow of sadness that had passed over her lover's face. "Matteo, I'm sorry; I feel so bad taking your son away from you. I know how much you care for him. But, it won't be for long." Laura realized that nothing she could say could blunt the impact of what she wanted for herself.

"Is there anything I can do to change your mind? Is there anything I can say? Just tell me."

"No Matteo, I'm sorry; I just need to be on my own for a while."

"I'll miss Michele terribly, but it is you that I need more than anything. I don't know what I'll do without you, but if it is something you must do, I will not stand in your way." Laura threw her arms around him and held him close. She began to weep and soon he cried along with her. It represented for both of them one of those poignant and sorrow-filled moments that carried with it, paradoxically, a joy that is resident in that aspect of living in which passion and intimacy are truly present. It is a moment that they would carry with them throughout their lives.

During the following months, Laura was involved in all the myriad details that she needed to attend to for her departure. These months probably were the most difficult time of her life, for she was pulling away from the one person who had been the greatest influence on her and whom she had loved like no other. Every time she saw him, she felt like her heart was breaking all over again. She had to use the utmost strength to retain her resolve to leave him. They avoided each other not so much out of anger or aversion, but rather to protect themselves from the pain they both felt so deeply.

One night while in the midst of this stress, she had a remarkable dream. She was rising from a bed resting on an earthen floor of what seemed like an old cabin. She was awakened by a strong burst of sunlight that came through the window. Suddenly, there was a knock on the door and before she could answer an elderly woman walked in. She had a face that looked like it was weathered by the sun and a dry hot wind. She had the most amazing deep-set eyes. The woman was holding something in front her like an offering. It was the skull of some large animal, and she was beckoning to her with an outstretched hand. Laura followed her and as they were leaving, the opened door revealed the stark unmistakable quality of a desert terrain. This apparition woke Laura up. The dream puzzled her until she recognized the woman - it was Georgia O'Keefe. Then Laura understood; all her confusion seemed to coalesce into a singularly vivid image. She realized now where she must go, the Southwest.

One evening as they were in bed, Matteo could tell that something was not right. "Laura," he asked, "is anything the matter? I can tell that something is bothering you."

Laura looked into his soft and endearing eyes for the longest moment. She then spoke, "Matteo, I don't know how to tell you this, but here goes. I've given a lot of thought about where I want to go, well I've decided. I need to go to the American Southwest." She decided, however, not to reveal the substance of the dream that convinced her; for, she knew that he would never understand; that this revelation would sorely provoke him.

When he heard her decision, something in him broke, shattering his composure and self-control. He rose out of bed began to shout, "I can understand that you want your own space and want to be free of me, but why must you leave me so completely and take my son with you. You are talking about moving thousands of miles away from me. What chance would I have to visit you? Have you no feelings for me at all? Want do you think I'm made of? Don't you know how much I love and need you! Do you care that little about me?"

She had never seen him so angry; it frightened her. "Please don't be angry with me!"

"Why so far way!" he demanded. "Why go off to a place so cut off from me and where I won't be able to see you or my son. I'm not your enemy."

A strange mixture of fear, shame and guilt filled Laura's being. With nothing else to tell him and unable to console him, she left the bedroom. Matteo slumped into the bed and entered the depths of a deep abyss that carried him into the night. He felt miserable, terribly alone and despaired of his own worth. He felt emptied of all desire. Neither the present nor the future seemed to be able to hold his attention. Once again, he was to lose the woman he loved. Once again, he was destined to face the loneliness that had haunted him after his first wife's death. But this time around, he was older and far less resilient. He had a son, and he would lose him as well. He was on the brink of a deep and formidable depression. He felt, in many ways, that his life was over. He had poured all the remaining vigor of his waning years into his relationship with Laura. It now seemed so futile.

From that moment, they avoided each other completely, spoke little and slept apart. They both did their best to keep their relationship as amicable as possible under

Return to the City of Eternal Light

the circumstances. Laura was deeply saddened, while Matteo felt beaten. There was little left for them to tell each other, for it had all been said. It was an immense strain for the both of them, but apparently could not be helped.

The American Southwest

The day finally came for her departure. Matteo promised to ship the rest of her belongings once she was settled, but refused to accompany her to the airport.

"Go if you must, but don't expect me to pretend to like it. Let's say our goodbyes right here," he said. "I will miss you both, terribly. If ever you need anything, you know where I am." He then turned to his son, who was standing some distance from them, walked over to his side and encircled him with his arms. He picked Michael up and held onto him tightly. He then spoke to him softly, "Michele, I want you to look after your mother. I love you dearly, and I will miss you. But, we'll see each other again soon."

Michael remained silent, for he was so confused, distressed and angry that he was unable to give voice to the chaos of his emotions. He looked deeply into his father's eyes, and took some comfort in the love and warmth they expressed. Matteo let him go.

"I'm so sorry," Laura said as she kissed him and walked away from him, with Michael in hand, for what seemed like the last time.

Although she felt hurt that Matteo would not go with them to the airport, she was relieved by this decision; for, she knew that his presence would make her leaving unbearably painful.

Michael, on the other hand, was sullen and had been so for weeks. Although both Matteo and Laura tried to explain to him the reasons for this dramatic change in his life, he remained unconvinced and blamed them both, but especially his mother. As soon as they boarded the plane, he said not a word to her. He was hoping that seeing his unhappiness she might change her mind and return home. The atmosphere between mother and child had such an aura of unabated tension and emotional darkness that the flight seemed to last forever.

When they finally landed and departed from the airplane in Tucson, Arizona, Laura immediately felt the heat envelop her. Michael was so shaken by these new and seemingly hostile surroundings that, in spite of himself, he clung tightly to this mother's hand desperate for some stability. He had grown into a fine young boy. His body was tall like a reed. He still had the delicacy of form and motion of a boy of eleven who had not yet reached the maelstrom of puberty. His face had the softness and subtlety of his mother, and the beautiful penetrating eyes of his father. Whenever Laura looked into those eyes she knew that she was making contact with a portion of the soul of the person she held most dear in her life. It brought to her heart an exquisite mixture of joy and sadness. It was the character of such feelings that helped fuel and maintain her creativity. She looked down at her son and recognized the fear and uncertainty in his demeanor.

"Michael," she began, "don't be frightened. I know that it must be hard for you to come to a strange place and to be separated from your father and your friends. I know that you don't understand what I'm doing; you'll just have to learn to trust me. I think that you will eventually like it here."

"What is this place? Where are we?" he asked apparently and willfully ignoring her comments. She could see that she had not succeeded in calming his anxiety.

"We're in Tucson, Arizona."

"Well, I don't like it! I don't know why you made me leave home. You just wanted to leave Papa. I miss him. It's all your fault. You make me sick!"

"Please don't hate me. I know how you feel, but you just don't understand." She tried to place her arms around him.

"Just leave me alone!" he yelled and moved away from her.

Awakening from a Distant Dream

His bluntness felt like a dagger that struck her in the very core of her being. She felt terrible at that moment and very much alone. She knew that she could not adequately explain her reasons for making the decision that she did, especially to an eleven year old. She also realized that she managed to hurt deeply the two beings she loved most in the world. Silently, she cursed her insatiable artistic nature, the terrible confusion and doubt that plagued her and her relentless search for truth. "Am I being an absolute fool?" she asked herself. There was no immediate answer to this question.

She rented a car, and for the first few nights they were in a non-descript motel not far from the airport. Eventually, she found a small apartment for her and Michael while she looked for some kind of work to sustain them. She had not lived in America for years; in many ways it seemed alien to her. It felt cold and inaccessible, and she felt so distant from it. She experienced her country much like an immigrant would, feeling terribly isolated, vulnerable and fearful of the future. On the other hand, she was aware of the indelible imprint that the culture had made upon her while she was growing up. It had a cartoon-like vividness with its sprawling and gleaming avenues of commerce. There was a kinetic vitality that seemed to be everywhere. The unmistakable frenzy that drives the culture and its people was a reminder of what had shaped her. She could not separate herself from these influences. She would soon find herself back in the fray.

In a few weeks' time, she found a job as a receptionist at a small legal office in downtown Tucson. Her boss, Sam Davis, didn't hire her for her qualifications, for she didn't really have any, but simply responded to some sympathetic chord and realized that she would learn whatever she needed to know, quickly. Sam had a remarkable facility for sizing people up; this was the main quality that made him a gifted attorney. He believed that

Laura's presence would have a positive influence on the office. He didn't know why he knew this would be true exactly, but he was confident of his assessment. Laura had that kind of impact on others.

Laura felt a great relief when she could count on a steady income. It freed her mind up enough to begin to think of painting again. She enrolled Michael in the local public school. Sometimes, when she looked at the boy, she could barely believe the physical and emotional changes he had undergone over such a short space of time. He was now old enough and ready to go to Middle School. He was tall and thin and would soon take on that comic awkwardness so characteristic of adolescent young boys and the stormy petulance that seemed to come bundled with it. Laura began to see the striking likeness of Matteo in the boy's features, especially the deep brown eyes, the full lips and the slant and shape of the jaw. This revelation caught her off guard and startled her; it was a realization that saddened her.

Those first months were challenging for Laura. She had to fight her battles on many fronts. She had to become accustomed to working for her livelihood. She had to put aside her art, at least temporarily, to keep herself and her son sheltered, well fed and healthy. It did force her, however, to put everything about her life in proper perspective. She began to realize how the sheltered existence of a student had protected her from so much of life as it is lived by most people in the world. She had to struggle with existence in its most elemental sense. In another sphere, Laura had to deal with Michael's hostility and anger. He saw her as the cause of all his loneliness and discontent. She had become a convenient scapegoat for all his adolescent confusion and turmoil.

In time, however, both had grown accustomed to their new environment. Surprisingly, Michael did not sustain his anger for long and began to make new friends

Awakening from a Distant Dream

quickly and to see the advantages of this big country he now found himself in. It soon became obvious that much of Michael's angst came not from a purely emotional source, but rather from the fact that the physical side of his nature had been neglected. In his new environment, his friends introduced him to hiking, bicycling, fishing and many other activities; activities that engaged his body as well as his mind. Unlike either of his parents, Michael had a very physical nature that needed to be engaged. For the first time in his life, he felt totally invigorated. The Southwest, with its wide panoramas, awesome natural beauty and balmy weather, called to him and brought to the surface aspects of himself that had been submerged. He discovered a new vitality and sense of self that he had not been aware of.

Laura was pleased to see this transformation in her son, who was moving rapidly into manhood. With optimism and hope once again rising within her, Laura finally resumed painting. She began cautiously at first. Her initial pieces were small and modest. Soon, however, her canvases grew in physical size to match the surroundings; her strokes became bolder, her control less evident. Her work had a new vitality and the detail of her work demonstrated her mastery of the medium. Her art ineluctably drifted away from her usual subjects and gravitated to experimenting with pure color and form. She also became remarkably prolific. It was as if a flood gate had opened within her and the contents of her soul were pouring out onto her canvas.

It was at that point that Laura had learned to become true to herself. She had passed from the desire and longing for expression into a full blown realization of that desire. Art had become a vivid medium for the life that lived within and through her. Her work became luminescent; it shone with her inner self. Laura had passed through a doorway into a world that Matteo had spoken to her about on so many occasions. "Now I know what he was talking about," she said to herself. The world that the psyche inhabits had become a part of her waking reality. She experienced a wholeness of being that she had never known or dreamt of. In this frame of mind, her thoughts naturally turned to Matteo. He was always there in her mind, very present to her. At times, she longed to have him by her side if only to talk to him. She did write to him, but her words focused on purely incidental matters that usually gravitated on their son, for she was reluctant to discuss matters of the heart. Michael, on the other hand, communicated religiously with his Dad often over the telephone. Whenever he finished these protracted and intimate phone calls, he became noticeably cross with his mother, for he still blamed her for his Dad's absence. Matteo wrote to Laura as well, but his letters were invariably brief and succinct. In this way Laura and Matteo attempted to find some safe and neutral ground upon which they could reasonably communicate. Such was the pattern of living that evolved in their new home.

A Strange and Unexpected Reunion

As Laura came to be recognized as an important Southwest artist and was well established, she moved to Taos New Mexico that had a thriving artist community. After she was living and working in New Mexico for a number of years, she had an opportunity to exhibit her new work at the prestigious Friedman Gallery in Taos. Once the proprietor had seen her work, he became an instant fan. He recognized the brilliance and luminosity that seemed to envelop her canvases. They were, in his estimation, "Both sensual and hauntingly vivid.

On one particular evening in the heart of the summer, Laura was to be the subject of a wondrous surprise. The sun was lowering itself into an orange-painted sky. She was standing in the back of the gallery when she noticed the figure of a woman who seemed strangely familiar to her. Her brain madly searched the archives for the faces of old friends and acquaintances desperately trying to figure out who this person was.

Suddenly, she realized it was Audrey Wrey, her high school art teacher; the one who had been her first inspiration. She approached Audrey, who was totally engrossed in one of Laura's favorite paintings, "The Shadow of Incipient Desire."

"Audrey," she said, "is that you!"

Audrey turned around and they looked at each other, both startled and quite speechless at first. They hugged each other deeply without a word.

"I can't believe it, I just can't believe it!" Audrey finally said repeatedly. "I looked at that painting then I looked at your name and I wondered. I just wasn't sure. Now here you are right next to me. I can't tell you how wonderful it makes me feel to know that you have become such a fine artist. Laura, this work is exquisite. It tells me not only about your acquired skill, but about your spirit. You certainly have become a master of your craft."

"Oh thank you," Laura answered. She did not know quite what to say, "You are in a large part responsible for what I have become. I can't tell you what an inspiration you were to me."

"That is very kind of you. There can be no finer compliment for a teacher." Audrey could not help staring at Laura. Of course, buried beneath her feelings, probably at the root of them, was her long suppressed desire for her former student. It was a desire that was never satisfied and never completely quenched. Finally, Audrey continued, "I can't believe that we are both here after all these years in such an accidental way. Maybe, it's not that accidental." She turned her head towards the painting she had just been admiring. "I have to have this painting."

"Take it," Laura said without hesitation.

"How much is it?" Audrey asked.

"I can't take any money from you."

"Nonsense!" Audrey responded. "I know about the life of an artist and what a hardship it can be. As for me, well I copped out."

"How do you mean?" Laura asked.

"I'm no longer a teacher; I got a job working as an illustrator for an ad company. I can't believe sometimes the crap my work is promoting. I always thought I could satisfy both worlds. But, I was wrong. I admire you Laura. No, I could say I envy you. You took the risk and here you are. You didn't squander your gift; I am so proud of you." After saying this she embraced Laura again. That embrace spoke a remarkable language of affection and desire.

"Don't be fooled, Audrey. You see only one result; you don't see the price I paid and am still paying." Laura paused, "We can't talk here; why don't you let me make dinner for you tonight?"

Awakening from a Distant Dream

"All right," Audrey answered as she wrote out a check. "I'll go back to my hotel in the meantime. Why don't you give me directions to your place?"

That evening, Laura was visibly nervous, awaiting the arrival of her old friend. The source of the tension was the sexual attraction that Audrey at one time felt for her. She was almost certain that some of that attraction was still there. She thought about how she felt towards Audrey. She just wasn't sure. She wasn't sure how much she could separate her own prolonged state of loneliness from the equation. It had been such a long time since she had an intimate relationship. She so hated to dwell on that fact; for, if she did, it invariably reminded her of Matteo and the love she had so voluntarily given up. These thoughts danced in her head without any satisfactory conclusion. She had a way of turning experience around in her mind, studying and surveying it through the prism of her perception. It was that insatiable hunger she had for understanding life in all its manifestations that drove her to do this.

These thoughts were disrupted when she heard a car pull up outside the house. She looked out the window and saw Audrey get out. Laura marveled at how attractive and disarming Audrey still appeared. She noted the grace in her movements and the way she carried her long supple frame. Suddenly, the thought came to her, "I must paint her."

As soon as Audrey came through the door, they embraced. Audrey was a little thinner than she remembered. She noticed subtle and not so subtle lines around her brown eyes. Those eyes still flashed and suggested an unmistakable passion and playfulness. The details of Audrey's features came alive to her artist eyes - the fullness of her lips, the high cheek bones, her small and slightly upturned nose, her hair with its natural tendency towards chaos. Laura took in all of this and began to see how this woman would appear on canvas.

Audrey insisted that she had to know everything about Laura's life from when they last saw each other. Laura proceeded to fill her in. She began with her first trip to Paris, her impressions of the city, her fling with Marcel, her relationship with Matteo, her son and, of course, the development of her art. As she talked to Audrey, time felt like it remained suspended in the air above them. She found that talking about her life in this way was therapeutic and revealing. She rarely had such an opportunity. Of course, she kept some aspects of her life and experience to herself, for they were not for anyone else to share. There is always a danger that when important aspects of living are spoken about too easily they can become trivialized and inadvertently give the listener rights that should never belong to him or her.

Audrey was totally engrossed and seemed to hang on every word. Finally, her curiosity got the best of her, "Laura," she began, "excuse me for being so inquisitive. Loving Matteo as you say you do, why did you leave him?"

Laura was a little taken aback by this question. "I've asked myself that question often. I don't think there is one single reason. It was almost as if our life had become too perfect, like a story book version of how living should be. I was growing restless and was unable to paint. I had lost any inspiration to create. It felt like something important in me had died; at least that's what was going through my mind. I think that he loved me too well, and I felt like I didn't deserve it." As Laura was speaking she grew more and more emotional. Audrey looked intently into Laura's eyes. She felt her love for this woman re-emerge stronger than ever.

"I'm sure you did the right thing, especially after seeing your work. But, I can imagine how difficult it must have been for you." Laura nodded quietly. "Tell me more about Michael."

Awakening from a Distant Dream

"Sometimes, when I look at Michael, I can't believe he's my son. I wonder where all the time has gone. He's such a challenge and a joy. I know I've put him through a lot; my life has been so chaotic. I do the best I can, and I don't think I've been a bad mother, but art is such a demanding mistress. I often feel guilty for taking Michael away from his father and all that he was familiar with. But that's enough about me. I don't mean to be burdening you with all of this."

"Don't be silly! I appreciate you telling me. I am flattered that you can confide in me. You and Michael have been through a lot, but you shouldn't be so hard on yourself. We all have to make hard decisions in life. I think you should be proud of yourself for handling it all so well."

"Do you think so?"

"Certainly. I think you've done splendidly."

"Thank you!" Laura responded, obviously touched by what Audrey had said.

They talked this way for hours. When there finally was a pause in the conversation, they were both amazed to realize that night had come and gone. Dawn was breaking through the window. They both laughed at this realization.

"Oh dear," Audrey said, "I guess it's about time I left."

"Wait," Laura protested, "I haven't heard about you. Don't think you can get away without telling about yourself. I'm dying to know what's happened to you. How much longer will you be in the area? I hope we can see each other again."

"I intended to take a flight out of here tomorrow, but I can reschedule."

"I'm glad," Laura responded. "Besides, there is a favor I must ask of you."

"What is that?"

"I want to paint you!"

A Strange and Unexpected Reunion

"You're kidding," Audrey said, both surprised and intrigued.

"No, no I'm very serious. Please?" she entreated.

"I am flattered. But I don't think we'll have the time."

"I think that within a week's time, I'll have it done. If not, I'd finish it later. What do you say?"

Audrey looked into Laura's eyes and realized at that moment that she was still in love with her. She was unable to refuse. "All right," she said. "I can postpone my departure for one week. But right now I do have to get back to my hotel." She found a piece of paper and scribbled down her hotel number, handed it to Laura and got up. As she was leaving, she kissed Laura gently on the cheek. A wave of excitement reverberated through her as she felt this closeness.

The Portrait

Laura was at the canvas that was still mostly empty waiting to be filled. Her eyes were fixed upon her subject reclining on the couch across from her in the front room. Audrey was draped in a long, flowing and loose-fitting white gown. Her figure was lit by the warm midday sun streaming through the two bay windows.

At first, Audrey felt awkward and a little intimidated. After all, the accomplished artist who was painting her used to be her student. She had remembered Laura as a naive and maudlin young woman with only the very beginnings of promise as an artist peeking through her self-consciousness. Now Laura had become an artist with a stature that had certainly eclipsed her own. Her life was a testament to a person of great courage and admirable will. Gradually, however, as she reclined, the seductiveness of the setting worked its way into her psyche, and she began to relax in a profound way.

As she looked at Laura, she took pride in the fact that she had been a major inspiration to her fledgling student. The attraction she felt towards Laura was still there. This made her a bit unsettled. The self-assurance she once knew had been diluted by life and its experience, for life is a great teacher.

Her musings were interrupted when Laura said, "Audrey, I told you all about myself, but what about you? What's happened to you over the years? I want to know?"

"Oh, dear, where do I begin? When we met - I'm sure you remember - I was very cocky. I actually thought I knew all about life. I was so arrogant. Now, when I look at myself as I was then, I have to laugh. What a pathetic figure!

"Soon after you left, and I did miss you terribly, I met Matthew. At that time I thought of myself as a confirmed lesbian. All that quickly changed. He had qualities I had learned to never expect in a man. He was warm, vulnerable and compassionate. And what a lover! I just couldn't get enough of him.

"Can you believe, we actually got married! It was good for a long time. I even found myself wanting a baby. All those feelings went against all my high-flown ideas about what it meant to be a woman. All my feminist notions seemed to have gone right into the garbage. The irony of all of this was that Matthew didn't want a baby. He was dead set against it. This difference was too big, and eventually it killed the marriage. It became a real mess, but I still love him and think of him often. We are only now beginning to talk to each other again."

"How long has it been?" Laura asked.

"You mean since I've been divorced?" Laura nodded. "It's been two years. They have been long and torturous years. It's amazing how one can get used to another person's presence. I've only just recently felt like I was getting clear of the confusion and indecision and finding myself again at last. And so, I came out here on vacation. And here you are."

At this point Laura put down her brushes feeling that her creative energy was spent, at least for the time being. Laura sensed that she was expected to say something at this point. But, she didn't know what to say exactly. She did know, however, that her feelings for Audrey had certainly changed. The next few moments were awkward and seemed interminable. Their mutual affection for each other, however, got them through it.

Audrey looked at her watch and said, "Oh dear, I guess it's about time for me to get going back to the hotel." She certainly would have hoped that Laura might detain her departure, but that was not going to happen. Laura walked her to the door. They embraced and Laura waved as Audrey got into her rental car, and as she was about to drive off Laura shouted, "Don't forget about tomorrow."

Awakening from a Distant Dream
Although Laura thought that Audrey wanted her portrait finished, she was not sure she would ever see her friend and mentor again.

Laura sat on the terrace facing east as she awaited the arrival of the sun. She remained still and was attentive to the myriad thoughts as they danced in and out of her head. She tried not to hold on to any of them no matter how dear or tantalizing they might appear. This was part of her meditative practice. When she had finished and returned to the house, her eyes fell upon the unfinished canvas. It was then that she recognized the passion she felt for Audrey. It was a burning feeling that was beginning to make her restless.

The canvas with Audrey's unfinished portrait was on its easel, unattended. Clothes were haphazardly strewn on the floor and left an unmistakable trail to Laura's bedroom.

Audrey's hands moved down Laura's body. They gently caressed her in what seemed all the right places. With both hands on the inside of Laura's thighs, Audrey gently spread Laura's legs apart and began kissing her. Laura let the sensations she was feeling take her. She surrendered to that kind of rapture that only intense physical pleasure can bring.

In the midst of this, Audrey stopped and brought her face up towards Laura, kissed her on the lips and said, "This is for you my sweetheart." It was not long before all these feelings cascaded into a voluptuous and immense orgasm.

When it was Laura's turn to give pleasure, she was filled with uncertainty due in large measure to her inexperience. But, once again, Audrey showed herself to be a skilled teacher. The afternoon melted into night before they both fell asleep in each other's arms.

The Portrait

Laura awoke early and seeing Audrey's body next to her reminded her of the night before. She had a sweet remembrance, but also felt ambivalent about herself and her own sexuality. "Am I really a lesbian?" she wondered to herself. "Could that be the reason I left Matteo?" These thoughts played in her mind without resolution. She arose and did what she so often did to clear her thinking, she painted. She worked on Audrey's canvas that she had moved to her usual work space.

It was many hours before Audrey awakened. "Laura," she called almost reflexively when she realized that her lover was no longer beside her. Laura did not answer. She got up without the thought of putting on any clothes. She was amazed at how much brightness filled the room. She passed through the small kitchen into the room where Laura had set up her easel. The room was filled with an artist's paraphernalia; the smell of paints hung profusely in the air. She approached the easel with a kind of religious conviction. She understood how sensitive an artist could be about a work in progress. As soon as she saw the canvas, her breath stopped.   There was Laura's rendering of her, but it was not her own image that captivated her but the emotional energy that was so crafted into submission on that canvas. There was the love and poignancy, will and conceit, hope and surrender all ensnared in a web of texture and color. The whole affect plummeted directly into her soul.

Laura came in from the outside at that moment. At first she felt strangely betrayed, but she ignored that feeling knowing that it originated within an artist's conceit. Actually, she wanted Audrey to see it. "What do you think?" she asked tentatively.   Audrey turned around somewhat startled. She did not answer but walked over to Laura and kissed her full on the lips. "It took my breath away," she finally said.

Awakening from a Distant Dream

Laura could feel Audrey's soft body against her. She placed her hands delicately on Audrey's breasts. She then kissed her softly on her cheek. They both fell slowly to the floor and made love right where they had been standing. Laura succumbed to a kind of passion she did not realize she was capable of.

Time passed quickly for these lovers as they were engulfed in the rapture of their shared intimacy. Time has a way of weaving its course without the smallest concern for human goals and aspirations. Audrey had to return to her former life, and it was also time for Michael to return from his vacation at a music camp in the Colorado Rockies. Laura was grateful for his absence during the beginnings of their love affair, but she was now missing him. Laura felt a little guilty that her relationship with Audrey had so occupied her that she had hardly thought of her son. This had really been the first time he had spent any time away from his mother. Both she and Matteo were both surprised to see that Michael had a talent and a thirst not for art but rather music. At first, this took them a while to get used to. They soon came to realize, however, that he had a natural gift and that was enough reason for that ability to be encouraged.

When it was time for Audrey to return to the airport in her rental car to catch her flight home, she dropped by Laura's place to say her goodbyes, They both had so much they wanted to say, but found it nearly impossible to say anything.

Laura finally, broke the awkward silence, "Audrey, I'm going to miss you. I'm so glad you have come back into my life."

Audrey, looking deeply into her lover's eyes, answered, "I think it was meant to be; I think we are meant for each other. Just remember, that this not goodbye. We will be together; I know it."

The Portrait

"I feel that way as well; although, I am less certain about our future."

Audrey was so touched by Laura's sincerity that she impulsively kissed her on the lips.

"Can you take the painting with you? I want you to have it."

"Hold onto it for the time being. All right?"

"Sure that will be fine."

"Walk me to the car. It is about time that I left."

Laura watched in silence as Audrey drove away. She had already begun to miss her. Ironically, she appreciated how lonely she had been once that condition of living had returned. Somehow, the loneliness now seemed deeper and more poignant. She consoled herself with the reality of her son's return. He was due to return in a few days, and she busied herself with the preparation for his arrival. Domesticity was not Laura's strong point but she took on those chores with a singularity of purpose that was unusual for her.

Soon, she was at the airport - waiting for Michael to arrive. Images of her son and his father moved through her mind. They were pleasant images that carried with them the benign burden of the memories of intense and loving emotions.   There came with them, however, the attendant feeling of longing for Matteo's presence. It was at such moments that she felt that she had really blundered. Somehow, she managed to let her own arrogance about her needs for personal development cloud her feelings for and appreciation of the beautiful person that was the father of her child. Now that he was no longer with her, she experienced the extent of the loss. "Why?" she asked herself. The answer was not forthcoming. Of course, this feeling had become terribly complicated by the beginnings of her love affair with Audrey.   It was practically impossible to reconcile these disparate realities. "Was it possible to love two different people with such intensity at the same time?" This was a question she was unable to answer. It became so confusing that she decided not to hold on to any of those thoughts but to let them pass through her.

In the midst of this intense introspection, the plane arrived. As the passengers entered the waiting area from the umbilical cord that attached them to the airplane, she searched what seemed like a tidal wave of humanity for Michael. Finally, he appeared. When she looked at him, she felt that, in some ways, she was looking at him for the first time. He seemed taller, more mature. His face seemed to have lost some of the plasticity of a young boy and took on more of the character and incipient turmoil of adolescence. He seemed more self-assured but more vulnerable. At this point, she could not separate her own perceptions from the emotion of their reunion.

Michael was indeed taller. He was soon to be fifteen and was beginning to enter the chaotic maelstrom fomented by his raging hormones. When he caught sight of his mother, his heart filled with happiness, but he took on an attitude of reserved demeanor. He was not going to expose his emotions for what they were - that felt way too vulnerable. Laura felt this conflict in his attitude, and did not understand the meaning. She did not know that he was beginning to separate himself from his mother. She simply contented herself on the fact of his safe return.

She immediately threw her arms around him, and looked at him intently. She could find no sign of hurt or tension in his body. She took his travel bag from his hand, "I'm so happy to see you," she said. She said this plainly with no emotional edge to her voice. Michael took it for what it was.

"You must tell me all about your experiences!" she continued as they walked towards the baggage claim area.

"Mom, it was incredible. I was surrounded by other kids who all loved music. The counselors were great. I

The Portrait

learned how to play the guitar, the saxophone and even steel drums. I don't think I ever knew what it really meant to be so turned on. I loved it."

"I'm glad," Laura said.

"You're not upset?" he asked her.

"Upset, what would I be upset about?"

"That I'm more interested in music than art; that I'm not following in either your or Dad's footsteps!"

"No Michael I'm not upset, as a matter of fact I'm happy that you are making your own decisions and following your own dreams. I wouldn't want you to pursue something just to please me or your father. It's your life. We're very proud of you." They hugged each other with great energy and tenderness.

As she reclined on her bed that evening, Laura thought about her life. She considered her loved ones: Matteo across the ocean, her love affair with Audrey, and her son Michael. Lost in her own reveries, she thought herself very fortunate to have what she had. When her thoughts wandered into the habitat of her parents and family, however, she felt the depths of her sorrow and loss. The past, of course, can be reshaped by the frailty of memory and the vividness of the imagination, but it can never be redone. This was the first time that she actually began to take some tangible responsibility for the relationship with her Mom and Dad. She saw that on many occasions her own behavior and attitude influenced the outcome of events. There were often times when she had the opportunity to be forthcoming, but chose not to. As an adolescent it was often easier to blame her parents for the confused feelings that she had about her own life than to look inside herself for the answers.

Not unlike her parents, she was reaching that age where she was unable to avoid her own failings. Besides, as their child, she carried within her a shared inheritance. She had tried to extricate herself entirely from her family, but could not. The truth has an unsettling way of demanding to be seen, heard and understood. This realization made her feel both relieved and sorrowful at the same time. She was awed by the enormous complexity that is so bound up with living. She began to cry not only for herself and her kin, but for all of humanity. "We don't have a clue," she thought as she fell off to sleep.

As her life became settled once again and she adapted to her son's return, it was destined to take yet another turn. One evening she got a call from her Audrey.

Audrey's voice was noticeably shaky. "Laura," she began, "I miss you terribly. I find that I can't stop thinking about you. I don't think I can live without you. I know that this may be difficult for you, but I have to tell you this. I quit my job and am planning to move to New Mexico. I need to be near you. I hope you can understand?"

Laura was at first shocked and bewildered by this wholly unexpected turn of events. Admittedly, however, she was also terribly flattered and happy with the prospect of having Audrey close by. "Audrey, I don't know what to say. Of course, I would love to have you close by, but what about your career - are you sure this is what you want?"

"I have never been more certain of anything in my life. I don't expect you to feel the same way about me, and I don't want to pressure you. You don't have to do or say anything. I can't deny what I feel."

"You will certainly be welcomed," Laura answered. "I am not as sure of my own feelings, but I do care for you. Let's just see what happens, all right?"

"Yes, absolutely," Audrey answered.

"Call me when you have all the flight information."

"All right, I will. You are very kind; I love you!" with that she hung up.

When Audrey first arrived, they both felt rather awkward and weren't quite sure how to behave with one another. Audrey was determined not to impose herself on Laura. For this reason, her behavior seemed tentative and somewhat distant. This rather strained relationship went on for months. This was soon to change.

One evening after Audrey had dinner at Laura's place, she asked, "Where's Michael?"

"He's staying over at a friend's house overnight," Laura answered.

Audrey looked steadily into Laura's eyes. "Look, I just can't continue this charade anymore. I am madly in love with you; I want to make love to you; I need to make love to you. Is there any chance of that? I have to know where I stand with you."

Laura saw how agitated Audrey had become. She got up and sat next to Audrey and put her arms around her. "Audrey you don't have to worry; I feel the same way about you." They were both overcome with joy and felt very much relieved. Laura stood up reached out for Audrey's hand and together they walked into the bedroom. They loved each other tenderly and completely well into the night and into the next morning.

"I feel so playful when I'm with you," Laura said as Audrey was curled up in her arms. The dawn was breaking through the window bathing their bodies in an exuberant light. "I feel so wonderfully childlike. It is such a relief to no longer feel confused about my own sexuality. I used to feel so guilty about what I felt towards women. It first started in the girls' locker room at school. I used to get aroused watching the other girls as they showered. I certainly couldn't tell the others what I felt. It made me feel so alone and perverse. The others thought I was just snobbish and weird. I did enjoy men, but it was never the same. I never felt completely satisfied. I could have orgasms, but emotionally it always felt like something was missing. I felt that it should be more, but maybe something was the matter with me. Does any of this make sense to you?"

Awakening from a Distant Dream

"Sweetie, what you just said could have just as easily come from me. It took me forever to come to terms with the person that I am. It took me a long time to discover that I can love both women and men. I thought that I was in love many times before, but this, this is the real thing. We were made for each other. I think I've known that ever since you first appeared in my class. I want to always be by your side." They held onto each other and soon fell fast asleep.

It was not long after this shared intimacy that Audrey had moved in with Laura and Michael. Michael was not too happy about having another person in the house. This feeling was further exacerbated when it became oblivious to him that Audrey was also competing for his mother's affection. It did not take him long to realize that Audrey and his mother were lovers. At first, this revelation had left him hurt and confused. "How could she?" he thought to himself. He could not get this thought out of his mind. The idea that she chose a woman over his father upset him deeply. He felt horribly betrayed and disgusted.

One afternoon when he was alone with her in the kitchen, he asked, "Mom are you a lesbian?"

Laura was totally taken by surprise at this question. It felt like she had just been struck with a blunt object. She thought for a moment, composed herself, then answered, "Yes, Michael I guess you can say I am."

"That's disgusting! How could you!" he exclaimed and ran up to his room. Laura did not hesitate to follow him realizing that this required further explanation; she did not want there to be an emotional divide between them.

She knocked on his door. As she did so, she could hear him crying inside. "Yeah," he said in a voice full of hostility.

"Michael let me come in?" she asked.

"Go away," he answered, "leave me alone!"

The Portrait

"I know you're upset. Let me explain."

He did not answer immediately. Finally, he said, "Okay."

She entered as he was drying his eyes. She came close to him and threw her arms around him. "Michael, I'm sorry. It must come as a shock to you. I'm sorry I didn't talk to you sooner."

"Yeah, how come you let her move in and didn't talk to me at all to see if it was all right by me. This is my house too! Were you afraid I would say no. I can't believe you did that to me. I can't believe you didn't give a damn about my feelings."

"You're right Michael. I'm sorry. Please forgive me?" With her fingers, she wiped the tears from his eyes. "Sometimes," she continued, "women fall in love with each other like they would fall in love with men. Audrey is very dear to my heart. I love her very much. I hope that you could learn to know her and at least like her. I would prefer that you give her a chance. But, I don't want you to be unhappy in your own house. If it's too much for you, then we should talk about it again. All right?"

Michael looked at his mother deeply and could not help but feel the intensity of her affection for him. He finally acquiesced. He needed some acknowledgment and reassurance from his mother, and got them both. He was assuaged. Curiosity then got the best of him, "Is that why you separated from Dad?"

Again, Laura was surprised by his insightful question. "You know Michael, at first I was going to say emphatically no, but to tell you the truth, I don't know." It was now Laura's turn to feel confused. Michael did not need a definitive answer and was quite accepting of his mother's honesty. After she left his room, she found herself in a very thoughtful mood. She meditated on the levels of complexity and the array of emotions that represented some of the myriad aspects of being human. She was also impressed with her son's intelligence and strength of character. Laura felt good about where their relationship was heading. He was finally getting to that stage of development where they could begin to see to each other as equals. She was impressed that the baggage she carried in her relationship with her own parents was remarkably absent here.

From that moment on, Michael tried to see Audrey without those filters of mistrust and jealousy that can so readily distort perception. Gradually, they came to see each other as members of the same family. Michael eventually realized that Audrey, rather than being a competitor, had his interests at heart. He came to regard Audrey as his aunt and called her that. The love relationship between his mother and Audrey, on the other hand, was something he chose not to think about. He simply accepted them both for who they were. This was a very liberating change of attitude for him and would serve him well in the future; for, he came to respect the rights of others to find their own way in life. He further recognized that there was more than one way to live. For their part, Laura and Audrey respected his feelings and remained discreet about their own shared intimacy.

A Time of Loss

Laura's life had entered a period of apparent stability. She had found a significant niche for herself as an artist and had a loving relationship and a family that she cherished. Life was apparently going well for her. She felt that she had finally found peace within herself and the world outside. It is at times like this, however, that powerful events can intercede and lead to irrevocable change.

It happened on a spring morning, April the twenty-seventh. Laura would never forget even the smallest detail of that morning. She was busily stretching some canvas on a portable workbench she had in the kitchen right below the large window facing south. The sun was characteristically bright making the entire interior space come alive with sharpness and clarity. Audrey was sitting at the kitchen table drinking coffee and reading the morning newspaper that had just been delivered. Michael was asleep upstairs in his room.

Audrey was speaking, "Laura, there is a story here about a new gallery that is opening up called Sunswept Galleries."

"Really!" Laura started to respond when the front doorbell rang. "I wonder who that could be?" she asked rhetorically as she stopped what she was doing and went to the door. When she opened it, a young man extended his hand, holding an envelope. "Telegram," he said.

Laura took the telegram and fumbled in her apron pocket for change, handed it to him and thanked him as he departed. She opened it hurriedly, feeling unsettled in her mind. She read the contents:

"Laura

Sad to notify. Matteo died 24 April. Deepest sympathy.

Awakening from a Distant Dream
    Angelina"

    She grew instantly pale and cried, "My God." She collapsed to her knees and her body slumped over on the kitchen floor.

    Audrey ran to her side, "What's the matter?" she asked.

    "Matteo is dead!" Laura shrieked.

    Audrey did not know what to say. Instead, she knelt beside her and encircled her limp body in her arms. Laura's body shook uncontrollably. Suddenly, her mouth opened up, her lungs filled with air and a terrifying scream came out. Audrey actually felt her body being pushed back by the power of that scream. She felt the emptiness Laura was feeling fill her. It made her entire body tremble as well.

    Laura's emotions suddenly seemed to grow tepid - succumbing to the utter coldness and despair that filled her. The world that so intrigued and enriched her faded away into a blank canvas. Part of her became unreachable.

    Michael was awakened by his mother's piercing scream. It took him a few moments to realize where the cry came from. He ran down the stairs. There he saw his mother and Audrey huddled together. His mother looked ghostly and frail like he had never remembered seeing her. She had always seemed so strong to him like a great ship that could survive and thrive in any storm.

    "Mom," he cried as he ran to her, knelt by her side and threw his arms around her. "What's the matter?" Laura heard his words but they sounded so distant. She could not make out their meaning. "Mom," he repeated, "what happened?"

    "Matteo, Matteo," she said and that was all that she uttered. The resplendent shadow of grief had encircled her like a shroud. It was a formidable grief born of a great loss. Its hold was tenacious.

A Time of Loss

Audrey gently took his face in her hands and moved his head so that their eyes could meet. "Michael, your father is dead."

He looked at her and heard the words reverberate deep within his mind. He instantly recoiled from the thought. He grasped her forearms in his strong hands and pushed her away from him. "No he's not; you're lying." He turned his attention to Laura, "Mother, tell me Papa's not dead."

Recognizing her son's cry for help, Laura was drawn to the outside world, if only temporarily. She threw her arms around him and brought him to her. She wanted to absorb him totally within her. She would have put him back in her womb if she could. "Michael, Michael, I'm sorry."

"No, no," he insisted, "you're both lying." He rose up and ran up to his room and slammed the door behind him. Laura lingered for a while at the surface of her consciousness, but realizing she could not do much good there, quickly sank back into the comfort of her interior darkness.

"What am I going to do?" Laura asked. "The only man I ever truly loved is dead and I am responsible. I killed him, Audrey. I broke his heart and all he ever cared about was my own welfare. What am I going to do?"

Audrey knew that Laura was not expecting her to answer such a question. Instead, she tried her best to listen and comfort her. "I'm sure that you are not to blame, darling," Audrey said. Laura looked at her with a wild look of distress and confusion in her eyes. Audrey felt the tenacious hold of grief and despair in that singular expression in a way that no number of words could ever communicate.

Eventually, Audrey coaxed Laura into bed with her. She held her in her arms through the night. The next day, Audrey helped her lover make arrangements to fly her and her son to Paris. Laura decided that she needed to come out from under the weight of her grief at least long enough to take care of the details of Matteo's death as well as look after Michael.

"Don't worry," Audrey reassured her, "I'll keep everything together here. I don't want you to worry about any mundane details. Just take care of yourself and Michael. Promise to call me when you arrive so that I know you are safe."

"I promise," Laura answered not sounding terribly convincing.

Michael had gotten by on even less sleep than his mother. His heart felt so heavy and broken that it would not allow the rest of his body to take its nourishment. He had become so withdrawn so quickly that it made Laura quite anxious about his state of mental health. She pressured and cajoled him to come with her back to Paris. She realized that a period of denial was probably healthy, but she knew that he needed to look into the horrible face of that reality squarely on. Eventually, he relented.

Audrey wept with the power of emotions that came from deep within her as she saw Laura and her son disappear into the belly of the airplane. The mask of bravery that she had so admirably adorned fell off of her as soon as she had a moment to be alone with the pain she stored in her gut. It felt like a knurled and terrible hand had its iron grip around her throat and was pushing the air out of her like a balloon collapsing as a result of a tiny rupture.

Renewal

The flight to Paris was uneventful. Michael sat through it without uttering a word. He was so deep within his sorrow that he was inconsolable. Laura understood and let it be, although her heart ached for him. She knew that she would eventually feel the sharp edge of his anger. It was very difficult for her to suppress the desire to ameliorate her own sense of responsibility by trying to assuage her son's feelings. In the meantime, she tried not to let guilt overtake her. It was not easy.

When they arrived at Orleans airport, it was raining. In spite of the dreariness, the city was as beautiful and alluring as she remembered it. While at the airport she immediately made some calls to her old comrades at the Institute. Laura assumed, given the interval of time that had passed since Matteo's death, that he had already been buried. She was not sure where Matteo was interned. She finally managed to get through to the Director of the Institute. In response to Laura's questions, he answered, "Matteo's death was a shock to us all; we never suspected that anything was wrong. We did have a brief memorial service for him here, but his body was sent to his sister Angelina in Ottaviano, as she requested." He gave her Angelina's number. Laura remembered Matteo speaking of his sister fondly and of his childhood memories growing up near Naples.

When Laura called, Angelina answered, "Pronto? Chi parla?"

Although Laura did not precisely understand the question, she deduced the meaning. "I'm Laura; I'm calling about Matteo."

Angelina had no difficulty speaking and understanding English and knew immediately who she was. "Laura, I've been expecting your call. I'm sorry about the telegram. I needed to get in touch with you right away. Where are you?"

"I'm in Paris with my son Michael."

"You must come here right away!"

"We are leaving this afternoon."

"Bene! Call me when you arrive."

She could not detect any upset or disquiet in Angelina's voice. This was somewhat surprising; she certainly could understand if the sister was feeling animosity towards her. She suspected that Angelina blamed her for her brother's death.

Laura was beginning to feel overwhelmed by feelings of guilt and inadequacy that did not even begin to touch her own intense and insatiable grief. She recognized the emotional state of crisis she was in, and was determined not to be so hard on herself. She had Michael's feelings to consider as well. Besides, she did not know what Angelina actually felt, but she would soon find out.

With Michael in hand, they flew from Paris to Naples. From there they took a bus to Ottaviano located on the Gulf of Naples. They passed through sweeping views of the sea, the rugged coastline and Mount Vesuvius. Laura was struck by the astounding beauty of the surroundings. Marvelous stone houses seemed to literally arise out of the bedrock. When they arrived, Laura called Angelina and got some general directions.

With some help from a local postman who was gracious enough to come to their assistance, they found Angelina's apartment. Angelina happened to be working in the kitchen and was peering out the westward-facing window that gave a view to the street. The sun was hanging low in the sky on its inexorable transit to the horizon. When she saw the silhouetted figures of Laura and her son, she knew right away who they were and immediately stopped what she was doing. She was not looking forward to this encounter – her feelings were a wild and chaotic mix of contrary emotions - and tried to prepare herself. She walked to the front door, opened it and stood there with her hand held against her forehead above her eyes trying to shield her eyes from the glaring sun. She was hoping that her English would be adequate.

"Laura," she called.

"Yes!" Laura answered.

She invited her guests inside. Her apartment was rather small but cozy, bright, airy and delightful. Laura could not help but notice a number of watercolors decorating the walls in the front room that were unmistakably Matteo's creations. Both women looked at each other intently. Angelina observed Michael, and immediately saw her brother's uncanny imprint on the boy's features and overall demeanor. She extended her arm and placed her hand tenderly on the boy's cheek, "Que faccio bello!" she exclaimed. She looked again at Laura and could not help but see the tenderness that was there and her own unsettled feelings and apprehensions were somewhat mollified. Their arms encircled each other in an embrace in which they each kept a bit of distance one from the other.

"Please, sit down," Angelina insisted.

"I'm so sorry," Laura said in a way that indicated she couldn't hold her feelings in a moment longer. "Do you understand English; my Italian is very poor?"

"My English is all right, thanks to school and the tourists that come by and visit here often."

"Tell me everything," Laura said, "I need to know."

"No, no, you and the boy must first rest, please! I insist. I know that you must both be exhausted. After that we will eat and talk; there will be time for all of that."

Laura looked at her son and saw the extreme exhaustion in his face and knew that she was right. "All right," she said. Their hostess showed them to a small room on the upper level of the apartment.

Awakening from a Distant Dream

When they were alone behind the closed door, they both went to bed. Michael crawled into his mother's arms. "Mama, I feel so sad!"

"I know Michael, but rest your eyes for now," she caressed his face with her hands as she said this. Feeling safe in his mother's arms, he soon fell asleep. As she was enfolding her fragile child within her embrace, she gazed around the room. It was simply furnished, and everything was bathed in a wondrous light that came streaming through the window. Through that window, Laura could see glimpses of the vast ocean as it collapsed into an horizon populated with voluminous clouds. She found this sight exquisitely beautiful and strangely comforting. Ordinarily, Laura could envision a painting in her mind that represented this scene, but not at this moment; for, a deep sadness enveloped her senses.

After Laura and her son had caught up on their sleep, they joined Angelina for a lovely pasta dinner full of all the flavor and delights associated with the cuisine from that region of Italy. Although Laura felt awkward and a little reticent; the same could not be said of Angelina.

She looked at Michael and said, "Michele I heard much about you. Your Papa talked to me about you. He was very proud. I see him in your eyes."

Michael looked at her gripped by an overwhelming darkness and confusion and did not know how to respond.

Laura broke through her initial reluctance to speak and asked the one question that had consumed her, "How did he die?"

Angelina looked at her for a moment before she spoke, trying to gauge the woman's feelings, "He was in his studio working when he suddenly felt dizzy. He gave no attention, which was usual for him. This feeling did not go away; it got worse. He went to bed and lost consciousness. A friend found him and rushed him to hospital. He went into coma and in few hours was dead.

Renewal

They think he had a very bad stroke. I did not get a chance to see him before he died. But, from what they tell me, it was better for him that he did not make it. If he survived, he would be unrecognizable – the damage to his brain was severe." At this point, Laura and Angelina were in tears and Michael became quite pale and suddenly left the table. He ran out of the apartment. Laura was about to follow when Angelina gestured to her to leave the boy alone.

"It is too much a shock for him; he needs to be by himself for a while. He will be all right."

"I suppose you're right." Laura tried to put her natural concern for her son aside for the time being. "Where was he buried?" Laura asked with a sense of unease reverberating in her voice.

"He was cremated?"

"Cremated!" Laura said feeling surprise and shock at this news. She was in such a state of disbelief that a feeling of unreality seemed to consume her.

"Matteo was not afraid of dying. He was very clear. He wanted his body cremated right away. He did not want a funeral. He felt that earth was for the living."

"Oh my God!" Laura exclaimed. She buried her head in her hands.

Angelina came over to her, sat down beside her and held her. "I know, I know," she said. "He left you and his son some things. Wait here; I will get his will."

As Laura sat there, she felt the awful weight and gravity of this reality pressing down upon her soul. She was face to face with the stark and unnerving consequences of her own behavior. There was no escape from the inevitable course of truth.

Angelina returned with the documents, sat down and handed them to Laura. It was in Italian and she looked perplexed. "Scusi," Angelina said, "I will read it to you."

"I leave to my dearest Laura the contents of my studio including all works, excluding the sculptures, finished and unfinished so that she might remember our

Awakening from a Distant Dream

love and possibly derive some financial benefit from them. To my sister Angelina, I leave my sculptures so that she might sell them and make some money for herself. To my son, I leave half of whatever outstanding assets I might have so that he might use this meager resource to further his own dreams and ambitions. The other half, I leave to my dear partner, Laura, who has profoundly changed my life for the better."

These words touched Laura so deeply that she began to sob with such intensity that she could barely find moments to breath. After a time, Angelina put the documents down. She continued, "Laura, at first I hated you for leaving my brother who loved you and his son so much. I saw you as a traitor and wished you dead. But now that I see you, I think I know why he felt the way he did. You have such a kind face. Your eyes are soft and speak of great tenderness and caring. I was expecting something quite different. I don't know why you left, but that is your business. Don't blame yourself; my brother always had a terrible stubborn streak and was always very proud. He was concerned about your welfare and felt the happiest when he knew you were doing well. He had his work, his love and his memories. I will take care of the details for you."

"I'm so sorry," Laura said. This was about all she could say; her heart was feeling so heavy and overwhelmed with a sadness that she had never experienced before. Laura appreciated Angelina's sense of loyalty to family and her obvious generosity. Angelina had a very expressive face and what she was unable to communicate in words, Laura felt and heard on a much deeper level. Laura fell in love with her not unlike the way she fell in love with Matteo. How she missed him. At moments, she was certain that the pain she felt in her heart was so loud and raucous that it could be heard by all those who happened to be around her. His loss produced a place of profound darkness within her that she knew could never be filled. It was a place even her art could not intrude upon without great risk to herself. It was a place where a deep and incurable depression can come from if great care is not exercised.

Angelina saw Laura's goodness and an unmistakable sense of clarity that well-developed artists can achieve - an attribute that Matteo had described to her so many times. She was a little chagrined at her own obtuseness. Seeing the boy brought with it emotions of pride and pain. The fact that her brother's fine qualities were reflected in another life lessened the acute sense of her own loss.

"I would like you and Michele to stay here as my guests. I do want to get to know you better. I know this idea may be uncomfortable for you. Please give it some thought."

Laura looked upon Angelina with loving eyes and an inner sense of admiration, "You are very kind. I don't have to consider; we would be very happy to stay here with you. Thank you."

Over the next few days, Michael's resistance to the trip, his stubborn anger directed at his mother and his refusal to deal with his pregnant grief began to grow less intense. He began to soften and his own exquisitely good nature worked its miracle upon him. There were probably many factors that helped ameliorate his depressed state of mind: the ineluctable passage of time, a change of place and, the glorious Mediterranean sun. At Laura's urging, he would go off on his own and walk through the town and ingest the open sky and great blue sea stretching to the horizon like painted glass. He was looking through his father's eyes as well as his own.

One day the miraculous happened. He was sitting upon a rocky promontory overlooking the ocean. There was no one else about. His eyes were focused on a great ship that appeared as a tiny speck on the horizon. The sun was setting, abating the intense brightness. He could feel the spray from the water cool his face. Suddenly, a breach appeared in the wall he so meticulously created around his darker emotions. He cried like he never cried before. The pain imprisoned in the deepest part of him was finally freed. For a time, he was terrified that he would not be able to catch his breath or that the extreme pain he felt would not subside. He felt that it would be an appropriate moment to die. Eventually, however, the last surge of anguish passed over him. Afterwards, he felt lighter than the air itself. Michael was himself once again. His body straightened and suddenly felt more fluid. His step became more buoyant. His face softened. His eyes could see again. More importantly, love poured into his heart - that same love that he had adeptly protected himself against. Now, he could let his father be present in him and no longer be a captive and prisoner of fear and anguish.

When he returned to his Aunt's house that day, both women knew that something extraordinarily good had happened to him. It made them very happy. They spent many hours together, the three of them, talking about many things. Angelina described at length her life as a child with her brother and family.

"Matteo was three years older. He was a good brother and very sympathetic, not like other boys his age. He was sweet and sensitive and always kind to me. As children, we often played down by the water. Matteo loved to create sculptures from the sand, as you might think. I watched him, fascinated by how he did it. Even strangers would stop and watch him as well. Some were so pleased and taken by his work that they even gave him money."

"Did he know then that he wanted to be an artist?" Laura asked.

"No, I don't think so. He just took his ability for granted. I really believe that he thought that his talent was nothing special. As a boy, he wanted to follow Papa and be a fisherman."

"When did all that change?" Laura asked.

"Oh, he tried to be a fisherman for a living, but it gave him no time to do what he really loved. He would disappear for days at a time. He fought with Papa all the time. Eventually, my father gave up, and let him go. It was not easy for him to do that.

"Laura, what did you see in my brother? He was older than you. This is a question I've wanted to ask you. You don't have to answer."

Laura was not surprised at this question, but was not sure she understood the reasons herself. "I'm not sure I had any clear reasons why I fell in love with him; I just did. His age didn't matter to me. There was just something about your brother I found irresistible. There were many things about him that I loved. I never met a man as accepting and vulnerable and as in touch with his feelings as he was. I never met a man who listened to what I had to say, and yet did not judge me. I can honestly say that he was the finest human being I have ever known!"

"Then why did you leave him?" Angelina asked abruptly not able to control herself, for this was the question that had plagued her for so long. "Excuse me, but I just have to know?"

Laura was afraid that this question would come up. All the feelings of guilt and insecurity that she held such a tight rein upon suddenly broke free and she began to cry uncontrollably. "I don't know, I don't know; it's complicated," she finally said when she could begin to contain her emotions.

Angelina could not help but feel Laura's pain. She got up, sat down next to her and embraced her. "It's all right," she said. "You loved him very much." Once Laura had calmed down, Angelina continued, "Thank you for being so honest with me about your feelings. I know how hard that is. I would have really been angry with you, if you simply told me what you thought I wanted to hear. Believe me I would have seen through that. You artists are all complicated, my brother no exception!"

The women both laughed and embraced each other deeply, for an indelible bond had been forged between them. "You know," Laura said, "I dreaded meeting you, but now I know I'm going to miss you."

"I feel the same," Angelina answered. "Life is strange. It can be so awful and yet so wonderful at the same time."

After two weeks had passed and Laura realized that she had to get back home, she felt reluctant to go. It was a feeling that she would never have anticipated.

As she was getting ready to leave, she turned to Angelina and asked, "Angelina, do you have pictures of your family, of you and Matteo and your parents that I might take back with me? It would be very important for me and Michael."

"Yes, yes of course," Angelina answered, "I will get them."

Angelina went with them to the bus station. The bus was there when they arrived. They all embraced each other deeply. They formed a vivid circle of warmth and tenderness. From the bus window, Laura watched Angelina's figure quickly disappear into the surroundings as the bus was leaving and tried to memorize her soft dark features, flashing brown eyes, the lips and jaw line that reminded her of Matteo but mostly the depth of her kindness and generosity of her soul.

Laura and her son remained quiet and introspective during the ride to the airport and sleep overtook them on the plane as they returned home.

Lovers Reunion

During her stay in Italy, Laura had often thought of Audrey. Her absence caused her to appreciate the woman she had grown to love with great intensity. She recognized in herself just how easy it was to take a person's feelings and qualities of being for granted. She thought about the unconditional nature of Audrey's love for her. She decided that she would never underestimate Audrey the way she had Matteo. The path to wisdom is often strewn with sad mistakes and human failings.

It was strange, she thought, how the tragedy of Matteo's unexpected death had so radically changed her perceptions about herself and the ones she loved for the good. When she got off the plane with her son, her heart was filled with happiness on seeing Audrey waiting for them. Her feelings of love had been, up to this point, confused and consumed by grief and mourning. Now that her preoccupation over Matteo's death had eased a bit, her love for Audrey again took the forefront.

Audrey, for her part, was so happy to see Laura that she could hardly contain herself. They held each other with both passion and tenderness. Michael was a bit chagrined, feeling left out. Laura, understanding this as only a mother could, quickly enfolded him as well.

"Laura, Michael" Audrey finally spoke, "please you must tell me everything."

Laura smiled broadly, "There will be time enough for that. First, let's get home; I have missed you and our home so much!"

Everything seemed exactly as it had been left. Audrey had taken meticulous care of the house, studio and surroundings. Laura felt the love everywhere. Michael, as well, was appreciative of Audrey's care especially with matters concerning him – this made him feel very much included. She had cleaned up his room, took care of his mail and kept his belongings in excellent shape. He remembered how hostile he had first felt towards Audrey, and how those feelings had given way to affection.

They spent the rest of the day sharing their experiences. For the first time, Michael also joined in the conversation. The three of them lived together in a very special way. They experienced an airiness of being with each other that none of them had ever known individually. They seemed to live without judgment, harshness, unkindness or anger. They truly respected each other. There were, of course, lapses into moments of discord, but these were rare. This was a remarkable environment in which real happiness prevailed. Laura secretly attributed this in large measure to Matteo's influence even though he was gone. She was living what Matteo tried so often to tell her was possible. At that time, she was too head-strong and dimwitted to appreciate his remarkable insights. She now recognized his true brilliance - a rare commodity in a world that has in many ways gone mad with itself.

The three of them lived together for another year; until, Michael graduated high school and was accepted into Arizona State University. In spite of the fact that his life was surrounded by art and artists, Michael's interests had since turned from music to science – his particular interest was astronomy. He always displayed a near insatiable curiosity about the nature of things. This was no surprise given the qualities of his parents. Although he had musical gifts, he was a scientist by temperament – his mind was analytical and he had a natural skepticism. Laura had the good sense to let her son explore and develop his own inclinations and talents. At least, Laura felt, he had learned to appreciate the beauty of the human spirit in all its diverse manifestations. She was very happy for him and felt very sad that she was about to lose him to the world she knew to be so capricious. Like any mother, she worried for him and his happiness and safety. These trepidations, however, she wisely kept to herself.

The night before his departure to university, Michael kept himself aloof and was in a state of denial of the fact that he would soon be leaving his mother. She understood his reluctance and went to his room.

"Michael," she began as she sat down on his bed next to him, "do you forgive me?"

"Forgive you," he said. "What do you mean?"

"For leaving your father and taking you away from him. I know how much you loved him?"

"Well, I did hate you for it at first. I didn't understand why you did it, especially when you said you loved him. But when I realized that Papa always encouraged you to follow your dreams, I decided that I should be able to feel the same way myself. I'm still not sure I understand everything, but I do know that you loved him very much. Mama, I love you; don't be sad, there is nothing to forgive. I do want the best for you like I know you want the best for me."

Laura felt that her heart would give way with the feelings of love and pride she felt for her son, who was becoming a man with such fine character. When she looked at Michael, she saw Matteo. She began to cry.

"What's wrong?" Michael asked feeling concerned about his mother.

"Michael, I am fine," she answered as she regained her composure. "I am so very proud of you. You make me very happy. I'm going to miss you." She held him in her arms with great intensity and tenderness.

Held against his mother's breast, Michael was given permission to be her child and be vulnerable with her. It was then that all his suppressed emotions broke through and inundated them both. Mother and son sat on the bed entwined in both body and mind. Moonlight glided through the open window and caste its pale luminescent

Awakening from a Distant Dream

hand upon them as they were ensnared within the magical world of the spirit. Eventually, Michael fell asleep and Laura left him there realizing that he would leave home a boy and come back as a man. This awareness sharpened the sense of her own mortality, but also grounded her in the eternal cycle of life and death, earth and sky.

Unity at Last

For many years Laura and Audrey's lives were filled with a sweet and inspired routine. On awakening at the beginning of the day they would meditate, sometimes together and sometimes alone. After this meditation, they went for a long walk and if the weather was right, would go for a swim. They had become so much an integral part of each other that they often did not have to speak in order to communicate. Thoughts had a way of drifting freely between them. They understood the essence of each other's point of view.

The brilliant light of the Southwest provided an endless inspiration and source of energy for Laura's art. At this stage of her development, she had completely abandoned conventional forms of artistic expression. She now attempted to capture the pure essence of color, light, shape and texture and the way these aspects interacted with each other and were always subject to interpretation by the mind of the observer. This expressed her belief that reality was in many ways a construct of the mind interacting with it. This was an evolving idea. When she was young, reality seemed to exist entirely outside of herself and was something to adjust to, struggle with and conquer. The mind seemed much more dynamic to her now. It was her feeling that the mind was busy crafting reality and not just responding to it. She felt that she was reaching the height of her powers. It was a time when she was very prolific. The work just seemed to flow out of her. Her stature as an artist grew and grew.

Audrey's outer life, on the other hand, was an expression of her relationship with Laura. She had no burning or consuming passion outside of the brilliant perimeter of her love. There were times when she felt dwarfed and diminished in the shadow of Laura's talent.

Awakening from a Distant Dream

She would occasionally feel the pangs of jealousy, especially when identified by others as Laura's partner and overlooked in her own rite. It was true that Audrey had abandoned taking care of some of her own needs in an effort to be with Laura. The fact of these choices sometimes was painful to her, especially at those times when Laura was completely consumed by her work. In spite of these occasional misgivings, Audrey felt that she was truly blessed.

One morning, after a restless night when these feelings kept her awake, Audrey returned to the bedroom and looked down at the sleeping figure of Laura as her naked body reflected the subtleties of the early morning light passing through the opaque skylight over their bed. On seeing her, Audrey was reminded once again of the depth of the love she felt for her partner. It also reminded her of how important love was to her. This was the life she had always wanted to live. She allowed her conscious mind to capitulate to this essential truth, and with that, undressed and got into bed with her mate. Laura was awakened by not only Audrey's presence but the love and warmth that radiated from her. They made love to each other with a sweet attention to the details that gave each of them pleasure, and a marvelous sense of grace that reflected the depth and breadth of their relationship.

One day while Laura was working busily on a new piece entitled, "Trail of the Sun Goddess," in which she attempted to capture on canvas the changing highlights and colors that the sun imparted on a small patch of her garden during its trek across the sky, she felt a sudden and sharply intense pain in her head of a kind she experienced many times before. It was not the pain of a simple headache. It was a pain that spoke of something far more serious. The frequency and intensity of the pain seemed to be increasing. She sat and waited until the pain subsided and continued with her work.

Unity at Last

She did not tell Audrey about this, for she knew that Audrey would insist that she go to the doctor. She did not wish to worry her. As for herself, she truly did not care. She had resolved to herself, since Matteo's death, that she would live life fully until life's end. She did not want the experience diluted by concerns of the practical; she had become so used to immersing herself in the immediacy of the present moment.

One Sunday morning, Laura awoke with the expectation that on this day she would finish what she came to regard as her finest piece. It represented to her the culmination of her exploration of the dance of color and light that played incessantly in the world and in her mind and vision. Audrey also had commented on how exceptional a work it was becoming. "Laura," she exclaimed to her once, "it's breathtaking. It is as if you captured the mystery of light on canvas. It gives me much pleasure to know I love the artist that created this masterpiece." Laura knew that this day would be a special day.

She had the house to herself. Audrey had gone to spend a couple of days in Santa Fe in pursuit of Indian jewelry that she loved. Michael was traveling through Europe having just graduated with a PhD degree in Astronomy and was embarked on his own unique path of development and self-discovery. As she sat by the canvas, she was remarkably driven to finish it. It was not her typical way of working. Her entire essence seemed to be entwined in that canvas along with her understanding of life and its wondrous textures. She was so caught up in this project that she moved the easel next to her bed so that she could rest between her efforts.

It was about dusk when she had finally finished. She put her brush down and gave out an audible sigh. She felt that she and that painting had somehow magically united with God, or at least her idea of creation. Her spirit had gone beyond the limits of her body, or of gravity for that matter, and now seemed to reside in a very separate and special place. She felt luminous like the star that gives life to its planet. She felt vaporous like the moon and wild like the wind. She was enveloped by a panoply of glorious emotions and inundated by the kind of understanding she imagined the Buddha must have felt. She felt great humility and arrogance at the same time. Her entire life and its meaning seemed lucid and brilliant like a finely shaped crystal. All these feelings passed in an instant and left her completely exhausted. She decided to rest and fell quickly asleep.

It was a sleep she would not wake up from; for, in the night a blood vessel exploded in her head, and she died instantly. Audrey found her body when she returned. A singular life had been drawn out from simple and troubled beginnings and progressed through extraordinary circumstances to shape an unusual, though also quite ordinary person. A human being had passed through the world who had left behind a wonderful legacy of love and inspiration that in some small way would touch many unsuspecting lives.

THE END